A Little Murder

Marie Stone

Olive Press

First published in 1985 in Great Britain and the United States
by The Olive Press, Flat 2, 92 Great Titchfield Street, London W1

© 1985 Marie Stone

Text and cover design by David Williams
Cover painting by Edward Hopper, *Night Windows* (1928)
Oil on canvas, 81·9 × 101·9 cm. Collection, The Museum of Modern
Art, New York. Gift of John Hay Whitney
© The Museum of Modern Art, New York, 1985

Phototypeset by AKM Associates (UK) Ltd
Ajmal House, Hayes Road, Southall, Greater London

Printed in Great Britain by Photobooks (Bristol) Limited

ISBN 0 946889 05 8 pbk
ISBN 0 946889 06 6 hbk

A Little Murder

A Little Murder

Chapter one

On Sunday night, in the pouring rain, Katie Brown wheeled the pram into the middle of the road. From the first-floor window, she saw it empty, sodden, forlorn. Lying in bed she wondered about the rights and wrongs of her action, but not for long. It was three o'clock and she was tired.

At ten to eight in the morning, instead of turning on the radio she went to the window again to see if the pram was still there. It was. Few cars used the short one-way street on Sunday nights and the traffic had not yet built up on this Monday morning. At twenty to nine on her way to work she wheeled the pram inside. The wrinkled yellow pillow had a sprinkling of black specks over it; the curled woollen shawl looked translucent with water; the entrance hall had a musty smell.

As she pulled the front door closed it was tugged away from her. The man from upstairs pushed past and strode away along the pavement. She shouted to him.

"Hey! I found your pram half-way down the street this morning. I brought it in, but it's all wet."

"How did it get out there, then?" he yelled.

"I don't know." Then in a firm tone she added, "The door's always open, I suppose someone just wheeled it out."

"Yeah, well, thanks a lot anyway."

He turned and set off at a quick march. The close-cropped hair, rolled-up army fatigues trousers and hefty boots should have made him look like a skinhead but he was too heavily built for such a youthful cult. He looked more like a genuine recruit.

'Thanks a lot.' He had sounded quite sincere. She chuckled to herself as she strode along Oxford Street. The casual arrangement of litter across the pavements showed that the dustmen had been. The shops were still closed. In half an hour or so they would start putting out the first rubbish of the day and the air would be full of diesel and human fumes again. As the cold air hit the back of her throat, she wished for the first of many times, even for today, that she did not want to smoke.

The pilastered façade, brightened with trailing greenery, gave an appearance of Palladian country-house splendour to the shop. A monumental exterior, it was well suited to the Faversham Company that supplied British royalty with rainwear and tweeds. Faversham was part of the Queen's English; defined by the Oxford English Dictionary as designating a garment of water-proofed cotton invented by Charles Faversham (1795–1868). The shop attracted thousands of foreign customers who were keen to acquire the most English of looks at prices that some true English folk could not afford to affect. Around the side of the fine edifice two simple wooden doors admitted the staff and goods. Katie went through these, up the backstairs and into a little office that served as a changing room. From the evidence of the coats, neatly suspended on hangers, everyone had now arrived except Diane. The staff had begun the morning ritual of sorting and tidying the stock. Katie combed her hair and put on some black mascara in one of the customers' changing rooms. The light from the long window reflected by three large mirrors made a critical start to the day: combed whichever way, her thin dark-brown hair looked as if it was positively balding at the back; around her chin and nose incipient blackheads that had lurked unseen at home became visible. Marian, a fifty-year-old, one of the 'girls' with whom she worked, had once said that one day she had looked in the mirror and all the wrinkles were there, all at once, nothing gradual. Katie peered closely in the mirror and saw wrinkles – a few more each day. Was there to be a day when the complete web would greet her? She smiled to jolly up her attractive thirty-five-year-old face, put her comb in her bag, hung it over her coat, and went to start the day, at 'Size 12'. Pamela was not far away among the '10s' and lesser-sized Favershams.

"Good morning. You look a bit rough, Katie, if you don't mind my saying so. Were you out late last night?"

"I just had supper with a few friends, but it did go on a bit late."

"Oh yes, that's nice. Did you by any chance see the play on television? About eight o'clock, I think it was."

"I don't have a television."

"Oh, I forgot. Anyway, as you were out, you might have had the chance. It wasn't very good. It was about women working in a shop – about two of them, actually. But all through it they talked about sex and abortions and things like that – are you still on the '12s'? Here's a couple for you – my mother said she was put off, she didn't want to watch it, but there wasn't much on. Sunday night's terrible. I don't think people really talk about those things so much. It was actually quite interesting in a sort of way."

They don't talk about those things here much. Katie had known three abortions, but no one in the shop was ever going to hear about that.

"Was it written by a woman? It sounds as if it may have been."

"To tell the truth, I didn't notice." Holding up three

9

hangers, with difficulty, Pam struggled to pull them free of the other garments on the rail. "These coats are a terrible muddle. Some people don't care, they just put them back any old how. You know who I mean, I suppose? She never tidies a thing unless Angela's standing right behind her. Angela ought to be more strict, don't you think so? It's not fair on the rest of us. I suppose it's because she's so young to be a manageress, really."

Diane hurried through the back door and into the office to change. She was the only one of them who changed completely. The others wore their uniform skirts home, although Angela always said, "strictly, it is against the rules." Diane did not care for the classic English look promoted by the store. As the youngest of them she cultivated a more fashionable look, striking and aggressive. As she entered the showroom, pushing her shirt down into her skirt, the uniform had the effect of taming her, it seemed so much more substantial than the remains of her preferred image – the spikey hennaed hair and pointed shoes. Her face had a youthful fullness and bloom, maligned by a slightly sour expression.

"Good morning all!" She passed by to beyond the '18s' and energetically shoved the merchandise around.

Katie met Diane somewhere around the '14s' and left to join Lotte, who was taking cashmere sweaters out of the divided shelves to straighten them on the glass-topped counter before replacing them, a pile at a time, to their allotted slots. Katie took out a bundle.

"Oh, but I have ordered those ones." Lotte's heavy German accent had a prissy overtone. Maybe she realised this because she laughed as if it were a joke.

Katie replaced the cashmeres although they did not meet her own standards of neatness.

"How are you this morning?" Lotte inquired without

looking up from a rumpled pile of cashmeres. She pulled label after label up towards her to read the size, not that she bothered to put them in correct order.

"Very well, thank you. How are you?"

"I am all right. You know, I have reason to be pleased. I can save quite some time each morning now. I wait a little way back from the people at the stop and then I can just jump on the bus as soon as it arrives, yes?"

Oh Hell: I hate people like you when I catch a bus. Katie was launched into an explanation of the good sense of the queueing system when Angela came over and asked her if she would mind going to first lunch today. She agreed and was told to go and have coffee rightaway. A coffee now was welcome. She wondered if she would regret the lack of it during the remainder of a long morning.

The first coffee drinkers of the day had the advantage of clean formica table-tops and of emptied, if not sparkling, ashtrays. The staff rest room on the third floor looked barren without the usual clutter of used plastic cups and dog-ends. For company there were the men – salesmen from ground-floor accessories and from second-floor off-the-peg and made-to-measure. Katie took a warm pliable cup of coffee and sat next to a tall thin man from made-to-measure, who had the *Times* folded open at the crossword, on his lap. She lit a cigarette, glancing to see whether to offer, but smoke already curled up from the bent head. When he noticed her, he took the cigarette from his mouth.

"Here, Katie, see what you make of 14 down. I know what it is."

"You know I'm hopeless. I'll never master it."

The clue to the crossword read: '14. I.J.K.L.M.N.'

On her way to the lift Katie heard her name called.

She went in to the telephonist's office. Carol was taking off the headset with its mouthpiece. Her assistant, Maggie, a black girl, sat behind a desk with a typewriter on it, reading the *Mirror*. Carol took Katie's arm.

"Hey, Mags, look after things for us for a while! You can have your coffee when I get back." Maggie glanced up over her paper. "Hello, Katie." She did not look up again for Katie's greeting.

Carol had Katie's arm and drew her towards the stairs.

"Carol, what is all this? Are we running away together?"

"Come off it, matey!" Carol let Katie's arm drop. "Seriously, though, I've got to talk to you. I'll buy you a coffee at the Italian place."

"Too late. I've already had mine. I've got to get back. What time's your lunch? I'm on early. I can see you then, if it's so important."

Katie expected a smile but Carol remained serious. "OK, I'll see you then. I'll come down to your floor."

At ten past twelve the Italian restaurant was empty of other custom. The emptiness, the dim lighting, their heads almost meeting over the narrow table – it all enhanced the conspiratorial nature of Carol's invitation.

"I don't know what to do, Katie, I can't tell anyone else – you know what the others are like. I mean, I like them all right, but, well, Angela is the manageress, so she would have to let on. Marian's so honest, she'd tell on principle, and she's nervous, right?" Katie nodded and waited for more. "Lotte's a creep, and she doesn't know what goes on in the real world, from what I can see." Katie smiled. "Pam's OK, I suppose, but I don't get on with her. She doesn't like me for some reason or other."

"What's this all about, then?" Katie looked up to see the waitress hovering. "Two spaghettis, Bolognese, yes . . . Yes, that's all, thank you." They sat back while the woman wrote the bill and put it under the sugar bowl. "Well, go on, Carol . . ."

"It's Diane. You know she wears all those funny clothes . . .?"

Katie relaxed, smiled . . . Another of those unimportant little problems like when one of the girls at work had BO and no one would break it to her. "They're not really all that funny, she's just interested in that sort of image . . ."

"I've heard a couple of things on the phone. Now I'm pretty sure – in fact, certain – that she's stealing. It's not only her, there are other people involved."

Katie did not enjoy hearing the news. "You're sure?" The pasta arrived. She felt much less hungry now and a bit shaky from apprehension or excitement. She stirred the spaghetti around in the sauce. "Hell! The other people – are they people who work in the shop?"

"No. They're her mates from outside."

"It's not right, though, is it? What are you thinking of doing about it?"

Carol sighed and said, "I've got to do something. I hope you don't mind that I told you?" Katie only shook her head, her mouth full of food. "Honestly, it goes against all my feelings to tell on her. If I go to management they'll call the police. Can't you just see that fascist security man, Greg, preening himself?"

Katie chewed on, then nodded thoughtfully. "All right, then. I'll see if I can drop a hint to her. I'll come and let you know in my tea-break, or tomorrow morning at the latest."

"Thanks, Katie. I knew you'd think of something. I know those bastard bosses, Sir Oliver Meeting and his kosher clan. They make fortunes out of us. Well, you know I hate the lot of them. But the fact is, she's gone too far." She saw that Katie was laughing, so she continued. "Well, we all fiddle a bit, but this is too much. And we'll be in trouble if it goes on." She leant towards Katie's grinning face. "That's right, isn't it?"

"I suppose so, more or less, I just like the way you put it: your muddled sense of values – or can I call them morals?"

"Well, it's appropriate: the world's a bloody muddle, let's face it."

"I'm facing it . . ."

"Look at my Adrian. He's too straight for words – but now he's the manager of that store he finds himself in trouble all the time. They lose about a thousand quids' worth of records and tapes a week." Katie whistled. "Yes, and most of it's the staff. It's the mates he drinks with."

"I'm glad he's been promoted anyway. Can you get a mortgage now?"

"We're going to try again . . ."

"Talking about morals . . ." Katie then recounted to Carol how she had put the pram out in the rain.

"Christ, you put the kid's pram out in all that rain! What if it had been nicked? What then?"

"It's all right for you suggesting I'm criminal, neurotic or something or other, but you'd find it really frightening coming home at that hour in the morning and finding the front door wide open. Not just ajar – wide open. I was afraid in case someone had broken in. Then I was bloody angry: they do it all the time. I have asked them not to." She stopped frowning and laughed. "I was pretty pissed last night."

They were both laughing when the waitress took the plates away. They ordered coffees.

"Those neighbours of yours don't understand words, so I suppose you did the right thing. You should have got rid of it altogether."

"Imagine being stopped by the police at three in the morning taking someone else's empty pram for a walk. I know it's a free country – but I'd be in the bin today."

Carol looked at her watch. "Ten minutes late. We are stealing time! I'll pay for these . . ."

"Don't be silly."

They each paid for their own.

At a quarter to four Katie had a chance to keep her promise. There was nobody else about as Diane came into the showroom. Katie walked over so that she was standing between the girl and the cash desk.

"Have you just had your tea?" Katie asked.

"No. I just went up for a cigarette. It's so dead today. It drives me mad when it's like this."

"I know what you mean. I've got a friend over in Jaeger's who says it's just the same there: rushes and dead patches."

"Oh, yeah." Diane looked around in a bored way.

"One of the assistants there was picked up for stealing – she got eighteen months."

"Silly bitch. I don't like their stuff."

She's looking very calm, not the slightest suspicion of guilt. Diane rubbed the side of her neck slowly, pulling the collar ribbing of her sweater down before starting from the top again.

"You don't like the stuff here, do you?"

"I hate it, it's dead. There isn't one thing I'd take if they gave it to me."

"Then you wouldn't bother to steal it?"

"*'Course not!*" She pulled the neck of her sweater out and let it go with a woolly ping, then turning her back on Katie she walked to one of the long windows, pulled back the net curtain and looked out on to Regent Street.

Katie told Angela that she had to go to the lavatory.

"You're all slipping upstairs today. I think you go up to have a smoke." She laughed at her own worldly wisdom. Katie stood silent. "No, seriously though, off you go then."

Carol had a posh, polite voice on the telephone. She smiled when she saw Katie standing in the doorway, listening in. As they moved away from the switchboard, Katie told her what she had said to Diane and the response she had obtained. "The story about Jaeger's was all made up, by the way," she added.

"Listen, you did really well. That was clear enough if anything could be. If she doesn't get the message and pack it in, she's thicker than I think she is. Right?"

Katie agreed, said she must dash, and then felt it her duty to make a visit to the toilet.

Half an hour later the cashier called Katie to the phone.

"This is Carol. Listen, I think she's planning something for tomorrow. Well, I think so anyway – let's just hope that I'm wrong. Anyway, that's it now – I've told Greg Adams. Oh, by the way, I haven't mentioned that you know anything about it, OK?"

"Damn! OK. Thanks for letting me know anyway. Bye."

"Is anything wrong?" asked the cashier.

"Oh, sort of. Hey, can I cadge a cigarette from you, please? Thanks. I really do fancy a smoke. If Angela asks where I am, tell her I've gone up to the loo."

There was no hint of summer left in the air, it was

profoundly autumn, the sky purple and the air navy blue as Katie wandered home along the wet black pavements.

I could not have made it any clearer. I couldn't have accused her – after all, she may be innocent. Katie smiled with doubt. *Maybe I want her caught? . . . Not a nice thought . . . But no one would ever know.* There was a certain excitement building up in her about the whole business. She found herself remembering the excitement of shooting at rabbits and pigeons – as long ago as Diane's whole life – during school holidays: some rabbit found still not quite dead, and then the necessary beastly human, humane thing – to finish the job. *No more blood sports for me . . . not anymore.* She imagined the heavy hand on the girl's shoulder . . . prison doors . . . she did not want it.

Water . . . Suddenly it was in her mind: H to O – H_2O. That was the morning's crossword.

Chapter two

The cluster syndrome, a statistical basis for it never rains but it pours and why things happen in threes, was Katie's description of the store being nearly empty one day and packed the next. Some days managed to average out to a smooth flow of business. Not this Tuesday though, for all morning they were kept busy with customers needing attention before the stock was tidy and in place. No sooner was one served than another was waiting, and each assistant often had more than one customer at a time. Everyone except Lotte had forgone their coffee-breaks, so as not to leave the others with even more work – and, of course, not to miss the chance of earning more commission.

At noon Katie got up off her knees, from where she had been pinning the hem of a coat for an American woman.

"Certainly, Madam. I'll go and check with the workroom for when it can be ready."

She put the raincoat over her arm, walked across the long carpeted showroom, up the low step to the cash desk where goods were wrapped and bills prepared. Angela, surrounded by staff and customers, was verifying a bill.

"Angela, I'm going up to the workroom."

Angela diverted her attention from those around her. "Very well. Go and get your dinner as soon as you've finished with your customer."

She's a bit flustered today, saying dinner again instead of lunch. A more careful choice of words had been consequent on her upgrading the previous year.

It was no surprise that the lift was occupied; she walked up the carpeted stairs, two at a time. Between the third floor and the top, the fourth floor, her shoes clacked resonantly on the worn brown lino. The workroom was spacious and airy, the only room in the building without net curtains. Eight large shiny lino-covered tables had tubes and cables for irons and steam presses festooned above them. There were sewing machines on treadle tables in the centre of the room. Tailors sat on the tables, their feet, comfortable in socks and sandals, resting on chairs. She envied them their concentration, the air of easy skill. Industry and peace filled the place. The tailors' comfortable attire contrasted with that of the rest of the staff working below, who, on their meagre wages, aped the expensive appearance of the wealthy whom they served. The workroom was self-contained. They made their own drinks up here, had their own washing facilities; they descended to the floors below only at the end of the day, when the time came to depart. Katie slumped on a bentwood chair next to Harry's bench.

"You couldn't by any chance give me yet another cigarette, could you? I'll buy you a pack for Christmas!"

"Of course, help yourself. I'd do anything for you, Katie. You're busy down there today, aren't you?"

"It's mad, like there's no tomorrow. You'd think rainwear actually kept the rain out. We haven't even had any coffee-breaks. Thanks for the cigarette. What about this hem?"

"All right, I'll do it for Friday. But tell them no more jobs for this week. From now on, it's next week."

"I'll tell them." She stubbed the cigarette out in the

tin on the bench and hurried down. The American woman and her husband were delighted; they took it as some sort of personal success. Katie took his credit card to the desk. *Why are the cards always in the man's name*? She felt some concern for this well-kept woman.

Half an hour late for lunch, standing beside the coat-rack, her arms raised to unhook her bag, she found that the whirl and tension of the busy morning was making her body tremble. Equally, she sensed an unpleasant dumping feeling that only sleep could remedy. But who could sleep in a rest room full of smoke and chat? Or in a cafe with its narrow benches and the smell of hot fat? The pleasure was in leaving as soon as the sandwich and coffee had gone down, a moment's contentment. When busy, food seemed neither too little nor too much. Back in the rest room, she could not concentrate on the words in the newspaper. Carol appeared at the door and, seeing her, came across.

"Well, it won't be long now." Her face was long and sad as she looked around the room. "Maybe it's the time of year . . . My mum was up to her old tricks again last night. Pissed as a newt, said she'd taken twenty pills . . . Her last hour, weren't we glad and all that. When I rang for the ambulance they said she'd already called! I hate her – I do, honestly – she's such a cunning old sod. She hadn't taken one bloody tablet. She's in there now, drying out. I could kill her myself – honest." Now she was laughing and Katie mustered a laugh before looking at her watch.

"Listen, I must go now. Maybe I'll see you later."

"All right. Cheerio."

The showroom was nearly deserted. The pale-green fitted carpet looked vast. Only the disordered garments on their rails told the experienced eye that there had been a rush of business not long before. Diane and

Marian were at one end of a rail putting raincoats squarely back on hangers in order of size. Pamela and Lotte were chatting to Angela and the cashier.

"Did you have a nice lunch?" Angela laughed.

"I went to the Greasy Spoon."

"You like it there, don't you?"

"It's just cheaper than anywhere else." Katie shrugged her shoulders, smiled and went to help order the merchandise. Marian looked up.

"It went dead almost as soon as you left." Pushing the hangers along with their shoulders, they made room which enabled them to put the rail of coats back to order. "Let's hope we don't have a last-minute rush. My sister's got two of her colleagues to supper tonight. I've got to cook a leg of lamb by eight o'clock."

During the afternoon customers were wandering into the shop a few at a time, the girls going forward by turn to serve them. Only Lotte, eager for commission, violated the tacitly agreed rota by serving out of turn. As the morning had been busy and profitable, the others allowed Lotte to try her luck – which did not amount to much – while they sat at the table and joked about her awfulness. Hot for commission and cool for work, was Lotte. The sales commission, set at one per cent, was not generous; still, as a coat cost over a hundred pounds the little extra usually brought the wage-packet above subsistence level.

By three the shop was full again. Lotte deserted one customer to try her luck with a second. Katie bade farewell to a French woman, who had not liked 'le trench', once on. She approached another French woman, Lotte's abandoned client who, left unattended, was about to make a horrible mess of the well-ordered coat-rack.

"Good afternoon, Madam. If you tell me your size, maybe I can help you."

The woman was pleased and within a quarter of an hour had selected a coat. She stood waiting for Katie to bring her package around to the front of the cash desk at the same time as Lotte came to present a cheque. Katie shook hands with her customer and they bade farewell in polite French. Lotte stood glaring.

Surveying a growing stream of customers that emerged from the lift, Katie became aware that the general hubbub reached a climax as the crowd parted. Diane pushed her way through. She came across to face Katie, pulling her by the shoulder in order to spit in her face. The spittle fell short. Katie stood rigid with shock that turned to anger. At first motionless, Katie then raised her hand to knock away Diane's arm. At that moment Diane let go, turned, and ran off and out of the back entrance. Half the visitors to the showroom had stood riveted by curiosity and surprise as the scene unfolded. The remainder purposefully went on with their shopping, one of the latter approaching Katie.

"At last! Can you help me, Miss?"

Katie went back to work. The woman was looking at her coated reflection when Angela came over.

"Please will you excuse us for a minute, Madam? Katie, I must have a word with you."

Madam nodded, not at all well pleased.

"What on earth was all that about, Katie?"

"I really don't know. I have no idea."

"You'd better get back to your customer. I'll see you later." Angela made her voice a fierce stage whisper.

Katie waited until Angela was occupied, then took a tea-break. The showroom was still full of customers. When Katie returned Angela was leaning on the cash desk talking to Greg Adams, the store detective, and to Jim, the back-door man who spent his working life in a tiny office watching the goods and staff coming and going.

"Katie!" Greg Adams adjusted his tie as she walked over. The backs of his hands, clasped in front of his rounded tummy, were freckled with red hairs. Always well dressed – the staff discount – there was something exaggerated about his would-be elegance. For a silent second she debated whether the motivation was vanity or insecurity. Short and stocky, he looked as strong as a gorilla. Katie took the initiative. "What was going on here this afternoon?"

He looked around before speaking. "That young lady, Miss Rufus, Miss Diane Rufus, was – in league with others – stealing from the store. We had a tip-off and so we managed to pick up her friends at the front entrance. Unfortunately, she must have been smart enough to observe us, because she ran away. Jim here chased her as far as Cork Street, but she gave him the slip."

Jim's broad grin showed his two remaining brown teeth, but he quickly adopted a more serious expression when Greg Adams looked at him. "The home address she gave the company is not, it would appear, where she actually resides. It was false."

Katie tried to look suitably surprised and impressed because she wanted Greg to continue. He paused as if he expected a more marked response. Having looked around again, he did go on.

"The police suspect that she is living with one of the men we arrested this afternoon and they'll be keeping a watch on the house – in Pimlico. Now, Angela – Miss Smart here – tells me that Miss Rufus said something to you on her way out. I don't have to tell you that if you have any information that could in any way assist me or the police, of course . . ." Katie was frowning at him. "No, of course, we know you, Katie – I don't have to tell you that. What did she say to you, though?"

"She didn't say anything . . ." Katie related Diane's

actions and her own surprise and anger.

Jim was grinning at her while the other two watched her seriously, as if they wanted a better story.

"You have no idea why Miss Rufus should do that?" Greg gently shook his head.

Stupid man. I've just told him I have no idea. "I suppose she didn't like me very much, and I happened to be there at the time. She didn't say a thing – she was in too much of a hurry."

"Yes, I see." Katie wondered what he saw. She looked from Greg to Jim, who instantly stopped grinning, pulled his sweater down and said he must be off. Angela and Greg turned and walked to the centre doors in silence. Katie joined Marian, who had a coat stretched out over the table to repin the hem.

"I won't bother to take this up to the workroom today; they won't start it until next week. What was that all about, then?" Katie felt comforted by the Welsh lilt in the woman's voice. "You know what's happened, I suppose?"

"Yes, they just told me."

"Apparently, Alex was knocked down in a scuffle at the main door. He's been sent home for shock. It's hardly surprising, I suppose – he's nearly seventy."

"I'm sorry, he's terribly nice." Katie was genuinely concerned about the old commissionaire's fall.

"Well, I don't know how much he helped, like, but they caught two of them. One got away – and Diane, of course."

"I am surprised, though. Diane hated the clothes here; she was always going on about it."

"Well, they don't keep them, do they? It's all sold. I can't honestly say that it came as a total surprise to me. Those clothes that she wore, there was something not quite right."

"How do you mean?"

"Well, I'm not saying she looked marvellous, but a lot of them were very expensive."

Katie believed Marian because she never said anything unless she was sure. Also, she had spent all her life in the clothes trade. Her last job had been fifteen years' service in a couture house, once famous, now defunct.

"Did you see them?" Katie asked.

"They came to me first, didn't they? They asked for Diane, said they had bought something from her previously and that they wanted to change a skirt. Then she came and took them over. They're very clever, they wait until there's a rush on. She must have given them a pile of stuff while they were in the fitting room."

"Then what happened?"

"There was a tip-off, so Jim was telling me. I expect they were known shoplifters."

The staff of the Ladies' Department seemed to be suffering from mild shock. At half past five, dressed for the cool outside, they hung together as a group at the top of the stairs – reluctant to venture, as individuals, into the cold damp streets.

Chapter three

Katie entered The Weymouth. Not to seem solitary, she sat at the bar to pass the time with the landlord's wife.

"Katie!"

Behind her she saw Laurence, an architect who lived in a flat across the street from hers. His velvet jacket matched the moth-eaten fabric of the seat upholstery. She joined him and refused a second beer. They had been close friends, sharing suppers and drinks, going to the cinema, or to the theatre, always knowing what the other was doing. For the last six months he had been busy and Katie had developed a preference for being alone. She looked at her watch and gulped down the remains of the beer.

"I must go, I'm seeing Andrew."

"Hell! Is *that* still going on?"

Allowing ten minutes for the water to heat there was still just time for a shower and shampoo. Feeling the rush of water rinsing off the suds, she wondered if the effort was genuine enthusiasm or an obscene ritual. After two years, the first flush of love was well passed. Andrew had always been married and always would be. They were middle-aged lovers. Promptly at half past seven the bell rang.

"God, this place stinks!" was Andrew's response to

the strong smell of ammonia in the entrance hall. Beside the soiled pram sagged a black plastic sack, dirty milk bottles spilling from the top and pushing through holes in the sides; this was a new feature of the place.

"Well, it's not me! It's my lovely neighbours from upstairs. I haven't had time to clear up."

"They're sluts."

Upstairs, he put his arms around her and kissed her heavily on the lips. She was glad that she had bothered to clean up her image. Flattered and pleased to feel his hair soft and clean, to smell the expensive after-shave, Katie, as always, felt a glowing contentment in his company. It brought with it the sensation of being a child again in that long-ago world that was orderly, fresh, warm, a sure base for fantasies and excitement.

Before taking off his trenchcoat he pulled a half-bottle of whisky out of his pocket. She had brought glasses from the kitchen and put them on the table. When a tapping came at the door, Katie opened it just a crack. The man from upstairs wanted to ease his way in. She stood firm. He tried to peer past her, into the room.

"Katherine." He pronounced the name as if it had an 'f' in it. "I'm very sorry to bother you, but we were thinking of going out and we were wondering, like, if, by any chance, you could keep an eye on the baby for us?"

"I'm going out myself later," she replied stoutly.

"Well, if you could just have a look in when you get back." He said it as if all was settled.

She murmured a bad-tempered 'all right' and was about to shut the door when he spoke again.

"We was wondering if, by any chance, you could lend us a bit of money? Just till the cheque comes next week, like."

Damn you! Without replying, she pushed the door shut, went to the table, took the purse from her bag, went back to the door, opened the gap again and stood once more to stop him looking into the room.

"I can let you have a pound."

"That's not enough, I was thinking more like five."

Behind her she heard Andrew stir.

"Well, I haven't got it. I haven't been to the bank."

At this he turned and bounded up the stairs.

Fuck you! You never paid back the two pounds from last week. You've got my tin-opener. And what about the milk and eggs you borrowed?

She smiled at herself for remembering every detail, heard a sound, and turned to see Andrew coming towards the door. He was a broadly built, large man. The heavy stature and paunchy good looks were enlivened by Glaswegian working-class aggression. The impact he made was softened by a genial confidence which was inspired by undisputed and deserved worldly success, and supported by a lively intelligence. As she closed the door she felt his arm around her shoulders and smiled broadly.

"They want me to watch the baby."

"I heard that. It's against the law, you know, to leave a babe a few weeks old on its own."

"I suppose you're right. Listen, I must tell you about the drama at work . . ."

Her story over, Andrew then provided a resumé of some recent facts about shoplifting in London. The subject came alive in grotesque detail, the cherished tradition of male story-telling. He was the producer of a weekly television current affairs programme and knew a lot of facts. His programme succeeded in being popular enough to matter. It was sufficiently committed in coverage of social and political issues to remain prestigious.

Andrew drew her closer to him.

"Shall we make love before or after supper?"

"You've really flowered, you old puritan. A year ago you could never have said that, you know."

"Well, a few years ago, I wouldn't even have thought it."

As he stroked her hair she recalled the diffidence with which he had faced simple love and sex – having a mistress, in fact – confused by keeping company with a woman outside the category of wife, quick lay, or plain wee whore.

"That's right." He emphasised his Scottish accent. "I shall be positively decadent soon – associating with you loose Southern women."

He took his shoes and socks off and led her to the bedroom. Outside, footsteps clattered down the stairs and the street door closed with a mighty bang that shook the whole house.

"You'll have to be quick – I'm starving hungry," said Katie, undressing at the same time.

"I thought it was your idea. It only takes three minutes anyway."

"Boasting again!"

A heavy chain rattled as the battered door to the upstairs flat swung open. The flat above Katie's had been carelessly modernised three months earlier, just before the young couple had moved in to brutalise it further. Andrew and Katie pushed their way in against the noxious aroma. There was a blend of smells: the occupants, the baby's nappies, food and filth overlain by cheap scent. The kitchen area was piled with dirty dishes topped up with cigarette ash and dog-ends. The wall above the stove was charred black. Dirty clothes were heaped on the floor. The bedroom was more ship-shape, but the smell persisted. Katie bent down beside the baby's cot. Brendan's eyes moved beneath their closed lids, his tiny face emerging sideways from beneath an eiderdown. She watched him stirring in his sleep and hoped his dreams were good. Brendan had well-defined dark rings surrounding the bags under his eyes.

She rose from her knees and quietly left the bedroom.

"There's a note here for you. Look, the writing is like a child's. Like a child who hasn't yet learnt to do joined-up. My eight-year-old could do better."

It read:

KATHRINE BROWN
If he wakes up the bottle and his nappie.

"Damned cheek! I've never changed a nappy in my life." She was angry.

"God, what a mess!"

"They're very young, they haven't been married for long and they've got the baby. He's out of work, so they're very poor – it must be hard for them."

"Come off it, Katie. It's no excuse. You're being soft. When Gilly and I were first married we lived in a damp basement in Notting Hill, but it never smelt like this. We were poor, but we weren't cadging from neighbours and off out leaving the children alone at night. I don't expect she even pays rent. Isn't she the landlord's daughter or something? He turned to survey the place. "It makes me sick. Look," he pointed, "you have to spend a bit to make that collection . . ."

On the floor in the corner were several dozen wine and spirit bottles, empty, full and somewhere in-between.

"I suppose you're right."

"Why do you suppose? Of course I'm right. Let's get out of here."

Andrew had to leave because the au pair was at home alone with his children, while his journalist wife was on a trip to the Middle East. In the days when it had been fresher, more amusing, more exciting, Katie had never really minded when the time came for him to leave. Now that she could feel sad in his presence she always hated his going.

"Go on, float up the hill to Hampstead. Apotheosis, and nip into bed with the au pair." She had hoped to conceal her feelings.

"Don't be daft." He bent to kiss her. "You know, I do sometimes worry about you. This is all terribly unfair on you . . ."

She stood up and was close to him. "I like your paternalism, it's a luxury." She stroked his cheek. "Don't worry your pretty little head about me." She held him fast.

Within minutes of his going she was in bed, the radio on and a glass of whisky in her hands. Closing her eyes she recalled him clearly, just as he had been in that instant when he turned on the pavement to look back up at the window. She wanted to know what his house was like. How it felt to go in through the front door. How it smelt. What was the bathroom like? The soap? The toothbrush? She wished to see the bed, the children, their arms, their legs, their faces. She wanted to peer at them to detect there some traces of him. She wanted to be able to love every detail of his life . . . his wife . . . "She's very like you in lots of ways." They were never going to become acquainted, or even to meet. It would be somewhat distasteful.

When she awoke she was in a fright. Someone was banging on the bedroom door to the corridor.

"Who is it?" Her voice was shaky but louder than she had expected it to be.

"It's me, Alan, from upstairs. Have you got any Disprin?"

"No. I'm asleep. Go away."

She heard him crashing up the stairs. A door banged and clanked. She heard voices arguing. *Talking about me?* It was three o'clock. It took a long time to get back to sleep.

Chapter four

While the kettle boiled she ground the coffee and it had happened again. One – just one – of the beans escaped intact from the terrible blades. She put it on the shelf alongside yesterday's surviving hero. It was one of those mornings when she had woken late and then decided to stay for a coffee, to be properly late.

"I'm sorry, I just didn't wake up, this morning."

"We thought perhaps you weren't coming in today."

What the hell did Angela mean by that? Katie was annoyed because she had always phoned when she had to be away, which was hardly ever anyway.

Straightaway she went up for her break. Carol saw her passing.

"Well, that's it, isn't it? I suppose you've seen Greg Adams strolling about like a cat with all the cream. He loves it all. It makes me sick."

"We knew what would happen."

"That's right. Some of his mates from West End Central are paying us a visit this afternoon. You do know that I didn't tell them about telling you, don't you? I had to more or less say that I'd only just found out myself."

"Yes, I know. But do you know what happened last, as she ran out of the shop?" Katie told her.

"If anything gets said at a trial . . . Well, we can say it was just a coincidence . . . Right? Are you doing anything for dinner?"

"I hadn't thought. I'm on early lunch-break. Come down at half past twelve if you like. We can think about it then."

"Hey, maybe you and I should plan a robbery. You're the sort of person I wouldn't mind being behind the barricades with, you know. Go on, help yourself..."

Katie smiled. "Well, I thought as you admired me so much you wouldn't begrudge me one cigarette. I'm not sure I should mix with bolshy anarchists like you, anyway."

"Oh, shut up! I've never met anyone like you for cadging fags, that's for bloody sure. See you later."

He seemed to be watching for her. The whole group of them observed her enter after lunch. She pretended not to notice, pressed her lips together to suppress a smile, looked down at the floor and made a swift bee-line for the office.

"Miss Brown, can we have a word with you, please?" It was Greg Adams. The other man looked as if he, too, was suppressing a smile.

"Certainly. Can I just get rid of these things?" She had a raincoat and bag over her arm.

She was annoyed with herself for wanting to look at her own face in a mirror. But there was no mirror in the office and not wanting them to think that she had made any effort on their behalf, she rushed out.

"Katie, this is Chief Inspector Anchor," said Greg, nearly standing to attention.

"How do you do?" She held out her hand. Chief Inspector Anchor took his thumbs from the slit pockets of his waistcoat. He took her hand. They were both grinning. She had to look away, so she gazed over his shoulder towards the windows. She could still observe his face and also that of Greg Adams who stood next to him, trying to keep a little to the rear, she thought, but the cash desk stood just at their backs.

"It's *Miss* Brown, isn't it?"

She nodded in reply. *He's playing the sheriff!*

"Well, young lady . . ."

"I don't like being called 'young lady'."

He looked surprised, his eyes widened and the smile left his lips. Angela, close by, looked upset – if not angry.

"I used it as a term of respect. May I ask what's wrong with it?"

"I'm not young and I'm not a lady. I'm a woman. Would you say 'young gentleman' to me if I were a man?"

By now she was wishing that she had not started on this one. Her face was turning pink.

Greg Adams shook his head and turned to the policeman. "She's a bit of a women's libber, is our Katie."

Katie scowled at him, shrugged her shoulders and waited.

"Fair enough, Miss Brown." The detective leaned back against the desk, crossed one foot over the other and put his thumbs back in the pockets. "Now, we don't think that you had anything to do with the robbery that occurred here yesterday."

"Thank you!"

"But we do just wonder if, by any chance, you had an inkling of what was going on . . . Did you, maybe, see something happening? . . . It could be helpful. Try and remember if there was any detail that might have made Miss Rufus suspicious, that might perhaps have given her the impression that it was you who tipped off my colleague."

Again she related what had taken place and that she knew no reason for it. "How did you know what she was up to?" She ended by asking Greg Adams.

He looked first to the policeman and then back to

Katie. "The tip-off came from outside."

"Oh, I see." *Secret sources, internal security, don't trust the staff . . . I see.*

Chief Inspector Anchor spoke. "I don't think we'll have to bother you again. May I thank you for all your help?" He held out his hand, which Katie shook. She was too embarrassed to look him full in the face and annoyed at her own embarrassment, irritated to find that she was joining in a silly game.

"Bye then, Katie." Greg Adams flourished his too familiar tone, then ushered his guest out. Katie watched to see the lift – it went up.

A few customers ambled around. Marian watched for Katie to resume work so that she could take her much delayed lunch-break.

"What was all that about, if you don't mind my asking?" Pam stood in the centre of the room surveying the customers before deciding whom to assist. "He looked very handsome, I suppose he's the detective, isn't he? By the way, I meant to ask you if you're not working late tonight – I know it's a bit late to ask for a favour – if you'd do a swap?"

Katie said that she would.

"Thank you ever so much."

"Don't be silly, it doesn't make any difference to me."

"No, thanks ever so much, really. I'll tell you why I asked. Bill's coming to London. It's bad enough getting back home after an ordinary day. I was hoping we could have dinner, nothing really special, that is – not really. There's a nice restaurant in Bromley – well, more outside it, really. Do you by any chance know it? Along the Chislehurst by-pass? No, well, it's along that way. They do a lovely steak and all the trimmings. They seem to get a nice crowd in. I'll do two nights for you."

"Don't be silly. Like I said, it makes no difference to me."

She felt positively jolly walking home in the dark. It did not take much analysing; it was the funny encounter with the silly detective. She was not pleased to realise she was attracted by him. His face was pale, almost pasty, with slight pock marks on the cheeks. His hair, short and curly, was fair brown – maybe grey. His glasses were the fashionably too big sort. His suit – just a touch too fitted – looked medium cheap, a bit flashy. The dark-blue navy made him look too pale, she thought. She did not admire the snobbishness of her own thoughts. Silly. She was smiling.

As she opened the front door Alan Remer came down the stairs, then stopped uncomfortably close to her.

"Katherine, can I borrow that pound now? . . . Thanks, I'll give it back next week. It's for milk for the baby. Katherine's spent all the housekeeping. We was wondering if you were going to be in later tonight. Like, it's my brother's birthday and we thought of going out for a drink with a crowd of them."

She agreed to look in on the baby. "Thanks." He bounded up the stairs two at a time. His tee-shirt had short sleeves that showed his muscles. His head looked bald. The hair was cropped so short. She smelt soap and sweat. The awful scent must be Katherine's. Her namesake was fat; bulges of flesh ballooned over her stiletto-heeled shoes, like a cartoon drawing. Her puffed-up face often turned bright crimson. Somewhere in the middle of the mass were the remains of a cute little girl's features.

What a cheek! What a mess! But her good mood continued. She grinned at the thought of them, her neighbours. Comfortably dressed in corduroy trousers and a Shetland sweater, she sat down on the sofa and dialled Laurence's telephone number. He was home, harassed, and about to ring her. Yes, he wanted to escape from his work. She had time to bring the Frascati from the fridge before the doorbell rang.

Laurence listened to the sagas of the neighbours and of the shop. It made a change to have stories to tell. As he drank, he became maudlin. The wine finished, they split the remains of the scotch.

"You're the exception, Katie. I find I can get on easily with you, I always could."

She smiled. "Well, I'm just a simple soul."

"I can't understand how you actually manage to like people."

She smiled again and inhaled the whisky fumes along with the gentle compliments.

"You go through life like an innocent. Maybe you just have low expectations, though."

"Thank you!"

"Well, I mean, how can you stand that awful job? Why do you do it?"

"Obvious: to make a living. It's not all that awful. It's all relative, after all."

He looked into his glass. "I can't cope. It's work and everything else. I hate everything." He sipped. "I feel as if everyone I've ever known has betrayed me, and it hurts. Except you – but you even put up with that couple from upstairs."

"It sounds awful. But it's rare all this, isn't it? You've been working too hard." She shrugged her shoulders.

"I lie in bed, I can't sleep – I just think in turn of my so-called friends and colleagues and the clients . . . and I'm in tears. I'm in pain. Do you understand?"

"It's not good." She could not look straight at him. She just wanted all the misery to go away.

He drank the remains of his drink in one gulp.

"Fortunately, I forget some of the time. You are my only friend; otherwise, there's no one else – only friendly strangers. That's why I love pubs."

She waited respectfully for any more self-pity. "I feel randy!"

"Oh, Christ, that's all I need. Darling, you know *I can't*." He took a deep breath. "Once you've decided to be gay . . ."

"Don't bother to go on. It's boring."

"When I first met you, you were always saying 'boring'. I thought then that it was very childish."

"Not as childish as being gay."

"I don't even think of women as sexual beings anymore. I can't go back. Anyway, I thought you saw that man last night."

"Sorry, I suppose that's the trouble. It unsettles me. It's the booze that's brought it on. By next Wednesday all this tiresome desire will have worn away. Even by tomorrow I'll be my boring self-contained old self again. It is a bit silly when you think about it, all the thrashing about and passion."

"Absurd." He tilted the empty bottle.

"But it always comes back." She gave him a wicked grin.

He stood now towering over her. "Well, you know what I think about it. He despises me and it's mutual. How you can go for all that Scottish masculine – football, mistresses . . . I won't go on."

"He was only having you on. Well, I don't want to end up one of those middle-aged women with only gay men as companions, thank you." As he walked to the door, she continued, "I get bored with all the gay alternative stuff; it was a fashion, and it's passed."

He opened the door. "If you've quite finished, I'll go and fetch some wine."

"Why don't you buy some chips as well?"

Chapter five

Fred Anchor had only had a few drinks with the 'boys' last night. It often bored him nowadays: the bullying, the laughing, feeling the drinks taking over. He actually preferred to come back to his flat and have a quiet drink in front of the television.

He stood, in his towelling dressing-gown, and with the coffee grinder held in both hands poured the whole load into the waiting filter paper, then he emptied the steaming water from the electric kettle over it. He must wash the surfaces. He liked it when the kitchen area with its white formica tops was clean. Now, everything was grimy – the black floor-tiles as grubby as the white ones. With the pot of coffee in one hand and a large cup and saucer in the other, he came around the partition into the larger room. The brown fitted carpet warmed his feet. He put the coffee things on a low white table, went to the door, looked on the hall floor in case the post had come. There was nothing there. He sank into the natural-canvas and chrome chair, poured, and drank his coffee. He had left his watch in the bedroom. Guessing it was about the right time, he turned on the small transistor radio sitting on the table. Exactly the eight o'clock news. Another spy caught. Those Bertie Woosters, all poofs and traitors: he should have known it all along, he supposed. Sex and money. He smiled to himself, but stopped thinking about the news. He turned the knob to hear some music. Out came the

Number One, a country-style song, 'Mighty Fine'. It suddenly dawned on him that he had been thinking of nothing but that woman (remember: *woman*), since yesterday afternoon.

As he walked past the front door he noted that were still no letters. He had no reason to wait eagerly for mail, but it always made him hopeful. From the door to his left, the bathroom, came the smell of soap and his body. He closed it, walked on into the bedroom. One entire wall was a cupboard. He opened two of the doors and pushed the hangers along the rail. He had worn the striped suit yesterday. None of the men in the shop wore waistcoats, he had noticed. He took out a tweed jacket (60 per cent cashmere, he remembered) with trousers that matched the fawn in the tweed, and finally a pale-pink shirt and the tie that went with that. It was nice to have things organised, things that matched. Then you did not have to worry about looking smart. He knew that some of the blokes at the station laughed at him because he wore different clothes everyday; 'Fred the suit,' someone had called him. It was easy for him. He did not have to worry about a mortgage, housekeeping, the price of children's shoes. He had only himself to think about and, so far, he had made few mistakes – a Detective Chief Inspector at thirty-six. Some of the men who had entered the Force with him were still walking the streets as plain constables. He had needed to distance himself a bit from the chaps, but it was worth it. He got on with them well enough. He did not mind the feeling of being slightly different. He put on white underwear, dressed, strapped on his watch and shook his arm for the sleeve to cover it. He was thinking about his friends, his colleagues, like last night, wishing they were less show-offs, more intellectual, less common, really; but when he was with grander, more middle- to upper-class people, then he felt working class and missed the easy laughter and the bit of madness that came from drinking with mates.

As he left he picked up two buff envelopes, put them in his trenchcoat pocket, closed the door, turned two mortice locks, walked down four steps and out into the grey light of a Maida Vale morning.

He drew the car in to the kerb and slowed down as he passed Warwick Avenue tube station. There stood a black woman, beside her a huge suitcase. It had been the same yesterday. It could be fun being a policeman – sometimes – you could satisfy quite a lot of curiosity; not that he was going to bother – today. He might, on the other hand, go and see that girl – no, *woman* – in the shop. He lit a cigarette and turned on the radio. Music filled the car. Stopping at the lights, he looked at a hoarding where there was a picture of a woman in army uniform, advertising a programme about the last war. At home he had a picture of his mother in the same uniform. That had been the most exciting period of her life, an escape from being a working-class housewife in Tooting, the 'house' a two-roomed floor. No wonder that she smoked. It had killed her in the end. Looking at her corpse, he had vowed not to smoke. Odd to do something so deadly stupid. For a long time, as a child, he had looked at men in the street expecting to see his father. Not that he remembered him, even then. He remembered his mother telling him that he was dead, killed in North Africa. He had not, he supposed, believed her. A car horn sounded behind him, he drove off wondering why all this old material was in his head this morning. Was it thinking about that woman that stirred it up? It did not seem right. He had driven like a robot and was surprised to find himself at the station. He parked on a cancelled meter – one of the perks of the job.

The main topic of conversation in the shop was still Diane and the robbery. As far as they knew, Diane was still free. Katie's thoughts were staccato: *I'm a middle-aged semi-failure . . . He's a vain, middle-aged, self-conscious policeman. He must be married. They probably live in Clapham, in a semi with a vinyl-covered cocktail bar at the end of the living room. Anyway, I'll never see him again. And I don't want to. And if I did, there's no future in it. I don't want to marry him, or anyone else I've ever known. He certainly isn't any better than the rest of them. In fact he's a good deal worse.* Still the embarrassing thoughts kept creeping in. Time passed quickly.

During the lunch-break Katie shopped at Liberty's, buying printed cotton for cushion covers.

She came striding into the showroom, the bag of shopping and her raincoat over her arm.

Something about her entrance made him laugh. He was standing, just as he had been yesterday, one foot crossed over the other, his arms folded. She stopped short. They were smiling at each other directly just for a second. She said good afternoon, went down through the showroom and into the office. Marian and Pam were sitting at the round table, at its centre an elaborate flower arrangement. As Katie approached, Marian rose to go for her break.

"Miss Brown, may I see you for a moment, please?" The detective's quiet voice carried clearly.

Marian sat down again.

"Certainly." Katie stood squarely in front of him. *He looks better today; yesterday's suit was too harsh, made him look anaemic. Today's outfit's a bit studied, but it actually looks quite good. Are the glasses different? Just a shade pinker?*

"How are you today?"

"Very well, thank you. How are you?"

"I'm well. I wonder if I could ask you one or two

more questions?" He looked around the shop. She looked around as well. He was still resting on the cash desk but now he leant forward, his face close to hers. "Actually, I don't really have any more questions about that business." She felt her cheeks warming up, and took a step back. He stood away from his perch, came close to her again, but with his back three-quarters turned from the women at the table. "I was wondering if you'd come out for a drink with me one evening?"

She hesitated. "Yes. Thank you." Of course she had known that this would happen, a dream linked to reality. It occurred throughout her life like a magic thread, the sun on the sea.

"How about tonight?"

"I can't. I said I'd work late."

"Over the weekend?" There was a faint, indulgent grin on his face.

"It's difficult. Some friends are coming from Italy and I'm not sure when they will arrive."

Now he was smiling openly. "Do you have a phone? I'll ring you next week."

"Sure." She smiled back at him, then added, "I'm not usually so booked up." They stood in a moment's pleased silence.

"What about the number?" Her confusion returned. "Your phone number." He said it gently. No one could hear, but Katie was aware of being watched as she went behind the desk, found paper and pen and wrote out her full name, address and telephone number, folded the sheet over and handed it across to him. When he had put it in his pocket, without a glance, he said goodbye and left. Lotte, Angela and Pamela all stood, as far away as possible in the lower part of the showroom, watching her. Pam had a big grin on her face.

"What was *that* all about, then? He looks as if he likes you, if you want my opinion. I was just saying to Angela he's handsome and he wears lovely clothes. He's not how you'd imagine a policeman, really."

Angela was giggling. Katie waited for the joke: "Well, you can always say you're helping the police with their inquiries. Seriously, though," she adjusted a suitably serious expression, "did he say anything about the robbery?"

"Nothing new. Maybe he thinks I'm a big-time criminal, I don't know." She did not like lying. *Why not just tell them the truth?*

"Oh, he's back again." Pam had stirred, thinking that it was a customer.

"I just want another word with Miss Brown." He stood at the edge of the step, turned as she joined him and together they walked towards the doors. There were subdued giggles behind them.

"Stupid," she murmured. He smiled quickly. She did not want him to think that she had told the others.

"I just wanted to say that I'm not married, in case you thought that I am. I'll ring you next week."

He left her feeling admiration and tenderness. It had been a sane and pleasant move on his part. *Maybe I should have told him that I prefer married men.*

Chapter six

Saturdays were working days – like any others – but they always seemed more relaxed. Maybe it was just the proximity of Sunday – a holiday, even for shop assistants.

When Katie came down from her break, Gina and Colette were sitting at the table watching for her. They sprang up and kissed her. She held a hand from each in her own. "What a pity you didn't come earlier – we could have had coffee together."

"We had coffee at Fortnum's, just now." She felt a slight pang that they had not even thought of her then. "We did not know that you are working today." The hurt was healed. "We are making a little shopping and this afternoon we go to the Tate Gallery, yes? Do you know it? Where it is?"

She explained, using their map and marking her own flat on it as well. They discussed shops, there were more kisses, and they set off to 'make' their shopping. Both girls wore jeans, American boots, cashmere sweaters and raincoats. Katie was aware of a certain curiosity from Pam, Angela and Lotte. *It's the kissing. They don't kiss girl friends. I'm an oddity in this place: not old or inclined enough to be a spinster like Marian and Lotte, nor young enough to go courting like Pam and Angela. Maybe they think I'm a lesbian. I hope not. I'm fond of them. I want to fit in.*

"Are those your Italian friends?" Angela asked.

"Gina's Italian but Colette's French; they live together in Sardinia."

Angela had a knowing look on her face. 'Ah, well,' thought Katie.

"How do you come to know them? If you don't mind my asking."

Katie explained to Pam, the others all listened. "I met Gina when she was working in London." She drew air in through closed teeth while she calculated, "About fifteen years ago now." Pam looked impressed by what must have seemed to her an historical fact. "We had rooms in the same house. She worked in a hotel. She came really to learn English but all the people she worked with were foreign, so I was her only English connection."

"This is it," said Pam. "Sorry, go on."

"Will you serve this lady, Lotte?" Angela looked back to Katie to continue while Lotte carried out the order with fussy little steps, shakes of the head and tutting noises. They all giggled.

"Anyway, we became good friends; she ended up sleeping on the floor of my room," now she glanced at Angela, "so that she could save the fare back to Italy."

"Well, this is it: after your expenses there's nothing left." A pause and Pam again said, "Sorry."

"That's right. Anyway, she met Colette in Rome and now they run an agency for holidays and property in Sardinia. They seem to do well, very well. They have a marvellous house overlooking the sea."

"I remember now – wasn't that where you stayed for your holiday?" With Angela smiling straight at her, Katie started to feel uneasy again. As soon as the next customer rounded the doors she stood up to serve.

Tamara was young, slender, beautiful and smelt as

pure and delicious as a flower. *It should be champagne*. Katie poured four glasses of the Italian plonk she had bought on the way home. She handed wine to Gina and Colette and then to Tamara who stood in the centre of the room, like a fashion plate: tall on high heels, elegant in an immaculate navy-blue trouser suit, a cream silk shirt and a long rope of real pearls. Gina and Colette, looking at the books, were both in trousers, neat and charming but not unlike millions of other rich, discreetly attired European city-dwellers.

Resting the wine bottle on the window-sill, Katie's attention was attracted by a car standing in the street below. Blandly ignoring the parking restrictions, it straddled the double yellow lines, stretching from one window to the other. The house juddered as the front door slammed. Alan Remer from upstairs bent to the chauffeur's window, straightened up, blew out a fine jet of smoke, threw a cellophane wrapper on to the pavement and marched off, leaving her an undisturbed view of the car.

"Is the car outside yours, Tamara?"

"No, it's my aunt's. We are living in London for the present."

"Is that where you're staying?" Katie asked Gina, who put an arm around her waist and hugged her to her side.

"Yes. Because, my dear English friend, we are too old to sleep on the floor any more times. Oh, I nearly forgot. We have a present for you."

Colette lifted Tamara's gangster hat off the pile of coats, then foraged about before producing a neatly wrapped irregular package.

Katie untied the string and removed the paper carefully, for possible reuse, an old habit. She held out the tiny basket piled full of sweets in shiny pink and mauve wrappings. "Thank you. I love them, you remembered. Come on, do have one." They all declined. Katie slowly unwrapped one and put it, whole, into her mouth.

Tamara was watching her. "Oh, so you love them too – my aunt as well. She misses them now. You find them only at that one baker's in Palau." Katie nodded. She was only just beginning to be able to move her jaw. "He uses real *mando* . . . no . . . almonds, yes, in the paste." Inside Katie's mouth the almonds were dissolving with the white chocolate coating, the luxury of the taste demanded that she recline on the sofa to do it justice.

Gina sat on the arm next to her. "I think you've made it nicer here." Katie offered gooey thanks.

"It's so central," Colette added. "We are staying in Highgate. It's almost like living in the country – the English country, of course!"

"Do you know each other from Sardinia?" Katie asked.

"Tamara's aunt is one of our oldest friends on the island. I think she was our first client."

"I think maybe so." Tamara helped herself to another half-glass of wine. "But now the things are very bad there."

"How do you mean?"

"The family of Tamara had the gates of their house dynamited. Everyone is afraid of kidnappings."

"We came to London for my aunt to have her baby; now maybe we won't return to Sardinia. But you can imagine, it's a very bad time to sell property."

"I can imagine. Has she had her baby?"

"Oh, yes. A little girl, just two weeks old." Katie smiled, thinking of her own aunts – all of them old women now.

"Well, my lovelies, shall we go? You're coming too, Miss Katie Brown."

"Where are you going?"

"The famous Key Club." Colette and Tamara were already putting on their coats.

"Listen, thank you all the same, but I won't come – I'm expecting someone to call." Gina and Katie rose together. They all kissed Katie in turn. She invited Tamara to visit her again, although she did not really expect it to happen. Their chatter was audible through the front door. The long grey limousine slowly drew out and sped off as she watched from the window.

The radio filled the silence, a play about a man writing a play. She had just taken out her needlework when the doorbell rang. It was Laurence, combing his hair back again and again with his fingers.

"I've been working solidly since seven this morning. I'll go mad if I don't get a break. Will you come to the Music Club with me? Please do."

"I've just turned down an invitation to a lesbian club. Now you come along expecting me to chaperone you to a men's gay club. Honestly!"

"I'll pay for the entrance, the drinks, for everything. Come on, *please*, Katie."

"Oh, very well. But there's not much in it for me, is there? Come in then for a minute."

She combed her hair and put on make-up. The transvestites at the Music Club were so much more glamorous than the genuine article that she felt obliged to make a small effort on behalf of her own gender. Actually, it was a jolly place.

Chapter seven

Pouring with rain, it was going to be one of those Sundays when the only other human voice was from the radio. Her head thumped and her throat burned. Back in bed she snoozed on until eleven. The newspaper was boring but she read it. There was nothing crying out to be done. No washing, cleaning, letters: a satisfactory lazy day. She considered changing her point of view and thinking of it as boring. 'It's all relative,' she told herself.

Last night had been fun. The drink had jollied her up, raising expectations inappropriate at a gay club, but pleasant. Where were all the passions now? She ruminated over a cup of coffee. Love, hate, fear and excitement were all much subdued these days. Pulling her dressing-gown cord tighter, she concluded that she was content to live like a cosy little vegetable. Oh, yes, the people upstairs with their troubles and rows provoked a response, a second-hand emotional life. It was the tranquillity of the Sunday morning that had reminded her of them. They had to be out.

Six o'clock, the blinds drawn. A tray of tea beside her, she sat at the table sewing. The downstairs door crashed closed. Their new habit was almost as annoying as the old one. The knock on her own door was gentle. Could she possibly keep an eye on the baby tonight? *All right. Why not.* He turned to join his wife who was already half-way up the flight of stairs, a bundle of babe in her arms.

A record was playing. She sipped wine and ate a cheese sandwich. It occurred to her that the music would obscure the sound of a cry from above and it was already nine o'clock. Food finished, she overcame her inertia and went upstairs. The bedroom had a new adornment – a poster of Nazi troopers, legs out, above the bed. Otherwise, the smell, the mess, remained the same. Brendan was whimpering and restless. She supposed that if babies had dreams, they were not real dreams. After all, how could they think before they used words? Dreams only in the sense of continuing feelings during sleep. But he was awake. His open eyes ended the speculation and she lifted him up – higher than she had intended. He was so much lighter than anticipated. He started to bawl and she thought of her freezing hands against his tiny body which was only lightly shielded by a tee-shirt. With one hand supporting his head and the other under his plastic-panted bottom, she walked into the other room, sat down and lit the gas fire. He was sitting up, supported, facing her and sniffling. *What to do now: why did I get him out of bed?* She circled the room with him in her arms, thought of turning on the television, decided against it, and made another circuit before returning him to his cot. Instantly, he was bawling again. *Maybe he's bored?* She dismissed the idea of his needing a fresh nappy.

A further attempt at settling him failed, so she carried him down to her own room, switched on a fan heater and rested him amongst the cushions in a corner of the sofa. It seemed to suit him. He looked content, his eyes swivelling as he attempted to take his bearings. Katie went on sewing, stopping every now and then to prop Brendan up again, not that he complained as he slipped sideways. It dawned on her she was hooked, the old mammal appeal had worked just as it was supposed to. She had become his willing defender. At a quarter to eleven she put her sewing down, stretched her back, then addressed him: "Listen, my friend, I'm going to bed now and so, I'm afraid, you must do the same. Whether you're inclined to or not."

Upstairs, she placed him, tummy down, in the cot. He quickly pulled his legs up under himself, like a foetus. His head turned to the side and was jerked by muffled sobs. On the draining board stood a dirty feeding bottle. She washed it out, careful not to let the foul water splash up from the dishes in the sink. There was no milk in the fridge, only cans of beer in the door storage rack where she had hoped to find it. Then she saw a bottle on the table, about one-third full but smelling sour. She could not bear to put it to her lips to test so she went down and brought up the carton she had bought on the previous day. Filling the feeding bottle used up all her supply of milk. After rinsing the teat she fixed it inside the lid, screwed it to the bottle and took the drink to the baby. He sucked it straight-away but the bottle did not lie on the blanket at the right angle to fill the teat. A bootee picked up from the floor made an adequate prop. He closed his eyes and went on taking rapid small sucks.

Katie settled into her own bed, warm and content. Suddenly, she was fearful that the baby upstairs might choke. She thought of going upstairs to check, hesitated, and fell asleep.

At eight o'clock in the morning she was woken by the telephone. It was Fred Anchor. She agreed to meet him, in a pub in Soho, that evening. She sat, her hand resting on the receiver. *Funny name, Fred – sort of dull and working class, quite good for all that. I wonder if he's embarrassed by it?* She reminded herself that she was very calm, not in the least excited: in fact, it felt like a mistake already! After the news came the song 'Mighty Fine'.

Walking to work she thought about Andrew. Maybe a new love would liven up their affair. A nasty thought, she decided. Fancy him being so eager – ringing at eight – quite flattering. But she was not going to look forward to anything developing and was annoyed to find herself debating whether or not to wash her hair. That just about summed up her level of thought, she reckoned: always today, the trivia of the present, diaries full of dates, jobs, rooms, days and days, years and years marked by shampoos and expectations.

Had there ever been a time when she'd had any real hope of fulfilling whatever it was that, most certainly, was never fulfilled? She was back to thoughts about the day and the night that was to follow; so it must always have been, she realised. *What the hell, I feel mighty fine!* The two walls of the narrow alley linking Charlotte Street with Rathbone Street gave a feeling of security. For a couple of hundred years people just like her had walked on the worn flagstones, their achievements now only fractions of memories and ways passed down via people. She was not going to have even that much impact, but she felt mighty fine.

Chapter eight

She did wash her hair and put on a skirt and clean shirt. It felt like an old-fashioned date. She looked at her watch. She still had ten minutes. She opened the telephone bill and her heart gave an extra and hard bang: nine hundred pounds and fifty-six pence – ridiculous. It had to be a mistake. Usually it came to around twenty pounds. The computer had a bad day, poor thing, she told herself. Putting the bill back in its envelope then into her bag, she put on her raincoat and left.

Fred Anchor was waiting. As she entered he stood up, looking gleaming clean and smart in a blue-grey suit. *It has been a long time since I went out with a man in a smart suit!* She smiled at the thought. Now she was glad that she had washed her hair and had not turned up in old trousers. Last time he had made her feel competitive. She wanted to continue a sense of superiority on his terms. Her own private values were not for him. She asked for a gin and tonic, he was drinking vermouth. He told her that he had booked a table at an Italian restaurant; he hoped that she liked Italian food.

"Open my heart, and you will see graven inside it: Italy."

She responded to his stare by murmuring, "Browning."

"Yes . . ." answered Fred, uncertainly.

"I love the food. I go to Italy nearly every year." He was then able to ask her more cheerfully if she was hungry.

"Nearly," she remarked brightly. "I've never actually eaten at the Lerici. I've seen it for years. It's funny, but it seems that living in the middle of town like I do, with hundreds of restaurants to choose from, it's always in the end one of about half a dozen old favourites."

"Yes, it is like that. Over the years I've met hundreds of restauranteurs. I suppose I could eat out free most nights of the week, but I prefer to go to places where I'm known and treated as an ordinary customer." It was said without a trace of smugness.

"You mean they don't have to tip you for their own good?"

He gave a sideways look "Enough of that, young lady . . . Oh, I forgot." They laughed.

"How's this for a computer joke?"

As he took the telephone bill he whistled. "You must have friends all over the world at that price."

"Of course I have, but the bill's usually around twenty pounds – maybe thirty in a heavy quarter."

At the restaurant they were given a table by the window on the first floor. The owner was wasping around them, all smiles. He flourished Katie's napkin in front of her eyes before placing it on her lap. They were offered aperitifs and grinned at each other over the menus. She was partly making fun of him but enjoying being spoilt; it seemed as if he knew it. He ordered cannelloni, she melon with ham to start with. They both decided on osso buco, the day's special, to follow. He was given the wine list and quickly ordered a Soave Classico without consulting her. It sounded fine after the gin and now the Campari. She stirred the red slick into the soda and ice with her fork.

"Is it good to be a Detective Chief Inspector at your age? It sounds very grand, I must say. I bet you're younger than I am."

"I don't think so. How old are you? I suppose I

shouldn't ask." Katie looked disapproving. "Twenty-eight at the most." She smiled at the compliment. He shrugged his shoulders and went on to explain about the eighteen months at the Police College at Hendon, coming to the West End – a tough patch with a high turnover of men. After two years he'd become a Sergeant and had been promoted to Inspector after another two. All the advancements, he explained, were about as fast as anyone could hope for, unless you had a degree. He made the word sound like an insult. Now he had been selected as a Chief Inspector, had been in the CID for five years and was hoping that: "My luck will hold out and I'll be a Superintendent in a couple more years."

"You must be a master mind." At that he turned to look out of the window before bringing his gaze back to her.

"It's not like you read about, you know, detective work. Lots of it's dull: routine, almost – like that business in the shop," he added matter-of-factly. "Otherwise, it's a matter of dabbling in the shit, if you'll excuse the expression, without it sticking to you."

"I don't suppose you need to be tempted by the wicked West End . . . you must make a mint of money quite legally." Katie said it cheerfully, but he still looked grave.

"I do quite well and the Force helps out with housing as well."

"Where do you live?"

"Maida Vale."

"Whereabouts?"

"I don't know if you know the area – off Warwick Avenue, not far from the tube."

"How very smart, nearly in Little Venice."

He shrugged his shoulders, but looked pleased. "Nearly."

They ate and chatted. By the end of the meal, over

madly expensive imported strawberries, some coffee and brandies, they were telling each other about their childhoods, both, in common, spent in South London. The good feeling, helped by alcohol, had them in total sympathy, each understanding what the other was saying without any undue elaboration. Katie was almost in a trance, which she realised suddenly when the owner surprised her out of it, looming above with his brandy bottle. "No, thank you." Fred put his hand over his glass and asked for the bill. She left him to go to the lavatory, essential if she was going to attempt the walk home. She giggled at her own face in the mirror before rejoining him.

They walked through Soho Square, past other Soho wanderers. She noticed him looking at people's faces every now and then. He also checked his car as they passed it. She preferred to walk home and he went with her. She invited him in, offering either whisky or coffee: "I think that's about all there is." She left him in the front room and went to the kitchen. They had decided on tea to ease the excesses of the evening. When she returned, he was examining her books and ornaments.

"I was just casing the joint, as they say. You've got some nice stuff."

As they sat on the sofa he put an arm around her shoulders. They kissed gently, the skin of their lips not wanting to part. When she rose to go to the kitchen for the tea her skin felt warm, she felt inspired. There was no thinking about what to do or what not to do; it was all just fine. They talked on, kissed, hugged and stroked each other. After about an hour he said, "I should be off now." She stood. It occurred to her to say, "You don't have to go"; but she didn't. It was all right as it was. They kissed and walked to the top of the stairs.

"Can I ring you tomorrow?"

"No, later in the week. Say Thursday."

Chapter nine

Tuesday was her day off. The electric coffee grinder rattled and howled; when the tone was a pitch higher she judged the grounds fine enough, let go of the button and unscrewed the top. In the first spoonful sat today's hero, a complete unscathed bean. She picked it out and placed it on the shelf alongside the two earlier examples. A miracle, she thought. When I have a dozen, maybe I should send them to the Pope.

After idling over her coffee she went shopping for food. Organic foods belonged to a past when her concern for fitness had helped underpin the healthy economics of the neighbourhood wholefoods shop. Nutritional value was no longer one of her worries and she rapidly filled a plastic carrier with freezer products and tins, and topped it off with cigarettes and a bottle of Italian plonk. The latter arrested the symptoms of any minor ailments and gave cheer.

As her lunch of baked beans simmered in the pan she warmed her neck over the stove, sipping a glass of wine. She was just about to sit down to eat when a knock came on the door. *It must be Remer. Damn! He will have heard the radio.*

Alan Remer wanted to use the phone, saying that the local box was broken and it was an emergency. The baby was trailing out from under his arm as he dialled with the other hand. A provincial orchestra was promenading through the minuet of a Mozart symphony.

Katie rose, clicked the radio off, then took Brendan from his father who nodded his gratitude. Some thick dandruff clung to the child's skull where it was lightly covered by downy brown hair. The head oscillated gently backwards and forwards. Katie steadied it against the palm of her hand. There was a rank sweetish smell about him – nothing high pitched, but mellow and foul. Brendan's hand grasped her finger and while she stroked the back of the minute hand she marvelled at the extreme softness of the skin, which was made of stuff so delicate as to seem unreal.

"Mrs Bresslain, in Welfare. She'll know who we are – you ask her." He needed to curb his anger. "Well, we were wondering if you could let us have any money . . . Well, couldn't you let us have some milk? Like, you must have lots of samples and stuff. It's for the baby because now we haven't got anything for him . . . Ordinary milk . . . Yes, I see." He looked deflated, staring at the receiver for a moment before replacing it. Then, flashing Katie a quick smile, "Hang on to him for a minute, I just want to go round the shops. Is that all right?" After ten minutes he returned clutching a tin of steak-and-kidney pie and a packet of cigarettes. He took the baby under his arm.

"You still haven't found a job, then?" It was obvious. Katie just wanted to show her nasty side.

"No, it's always the same." He sounded cheerful. "Any jobs that come up, by the time they've deducted tax and all that, you end up with the same as the Social."

Katie went to open the door for him.

"Mind you, my wife gets depressed. I left her up there now – crying." He walked to the door, the baby flapping.

"Listen, ask her to come down, if she wants to. She can have some tea later. It's my day off."

"All right, then." She heard his heavy tread ascending the stairs. Still holding the door open, she wondered quite why she had made the offer. There was the familiar sense of relief at his going – everything left intact. His manner was threatening, ominously shifting from foot to foot as if repressing something more than energy: his smell of soap and sweat hung in the room as she spooned up the cold beans.

Katherine's scent was stronger than her personality. She entered, seeming not to want to be there at all. They drank tea. When footsteps sounded from above, Katie smiled as her namesake stammered apologies for the racket they sometimes made. Her accent was refined in contrast to her husband's.

"We didn't have our first row until after we were married. I didn't really know Alan very well, I suppose. Before we got married, that is."

"Really?" said Katie after a pause.

"I became pregnant, so we had to get married. I wouldn't have liked to have an abortion or something like that."

Katie nodded sympathetically, rather liking the woman for being so open, especially as she was so nervous.

"I think he gets frustrated now, what with having the baby and not having a job. Being stuck here so much. I know I'm a difficult person to be with."

Katie frowned in disbelief.

"I am, you know. I can only sleep for about three hours a night. I've always been like that."

"Really?"

"But now I get depressed as well, since I've had the baby. Maybe it's the flat and being in so much. I hope you don't mind me telling you all this?"

"Of course not."

"I don't know anyone who lives around here. I used

61

to have a few friends from school, when I lived at home with my parents in Morden. But it's so far away, now."

"You were lucky, anyway, that your father could let you have the flat."

"Yes, I suppose so." She did not sound convinced.

"It's normal to be depressed after having a baby, isn't it? Didn't the doctors or Welfare people say anything about it?"

"I never went to any of those classes before he was born, so I don't know. They've got some now, on parenthood. Do you think I should go?"

"Yes, why not? At least you'd meet other mothers who might have the same problems. Look, wait a minute, I think I've got a book about it." She knelt to examine the bottom shelf that held the larger books. "Yes, here." She opened the big floppy book about women's health written by the Boston Women's Health Collective. "Here's a piece about post-natal depression." She handed the open book to the woman.

"You've got a lot of books. You must read a lot." She looked from the shelves to the book on her lap, opened it at a few pages, but within the minute she'd put it down beside her on the sofa.

"I read a bit. I don't know why I keep them all, really. I don't like having them around, it's just difficult to throw books away. If you ever want to borrow one, you're very welcome."

"Thanks, but I only read magazines. Do you hear a lot of noise from us?"

"Sometimes, yes."

"He gets violent. Look at my eye. I suppose you've seen it already." A week ago it had been black, now it was just pink and puffy.

"It looks as if it's nearly cleared up." Katie tried to sound positive.

"He just goes mad sometimes. There's nothing I can

do to stop him, he's very strong. He never touches the baby, though. He's not a bad man. It's because he's young. Too young to be married, I suppose." Before Katie was ready with a reply, the woman asked her if she had ever been married.

"No, I never felt the need to be. I once lived with someone for two or three years, but I got fed up with it. I have a few lovers on and off nowadays, but it suits me to live on my own." Katie was surprised by her own frankness. Katherine looked surprised as well. She was maybe shocked at what she was hearing. One way or the other, Katie was not really bothered.

Katherine rose clutching the book, thanked Katie for the tea and left. The scent lingered. It reminded Katie that her sensitivity to smells was increasing day by day.

Clearing up the tea things led to cleaning the kitchen. One thing after another: the front room, the bedroom and finally the corridor and stairs. The sun had shone that day and shown up every speck of dust. Two hours later, hot and with a dry throat, she sat down to admire her sparkling habitation. *Nest-building*. She thought of cotton covers still to be finished, rugs to be cleaned, the blinds washed, the whole place transformed before the New Year. Somewhere in her mind was the thought that he would be coming to visit. Not, of course, she told herself, that it mattered to her.

After taking a shower she was dressing when Laurence telephoned. He needed to cancel their annual viewing of *Les Enfants du Paradis* at the Academy Cinema – he was exhausted by too much work. Katie did not mind because she knew it was an important job for him, a huge restoration in Devon. Instead, she took out the sewing to make herself do the cutting out. She hated this part but it was of fundamental importance if the entire patchwork was to succeed. Although it was too dark to work, she remained seated for a while. In place of the windows, patches of light made a pair of abstract pictures, thick bands of indigo sky with a confusion of tiles, masonry and yellow-bright windows below. A street light gave the whole a sodium-scorched glow.

Chapter ten

"Hello. You sound half-asleep."

"Maybe that's because I *am* half-asleep. What's the time?"

"Ten to eight."

"You sound altogether too bright."

"I'm all right, I suppose. Can I see you this evening?"

"No." It was said with feelings of guilt. "I'm busy this evening." (Every Wednesday, she thought of adding, but did not.)

"Are you busy tomorrow evening?" he asked gravely.

"No, I'm not."

"Well, can I see you then? What time? I'll pick you up about half past six. I should be finished by then . . . I'll see you then."

She agreed. There was nothing to add. After a silence she put the phone down. Setting off to the kitchen she nearly tripped over the Boston Women's Health Book, left outside her door. *That was quick. I bet she didn't read it. Maybe she went cross-eyed at the bits about masturbation and lesbianism. In which case they must have a very low opinion of me now!*

Katie felt profoundly sensual. Kissed the escapee bean of the day. The walk to work sustained the feeling of well-being. She would ring Andrew later that morning.

The staff call box always seemed to be out of order.

"Angela, I'm sorry, but I really have to make two calls this morning. They're both important."

Using the shop phone was never popular with the management, but it was worth a small grovel. Today, her own affairs were uppermost, the chit-chat and work only a backdrop. At ten she rang the telephone accounts. The man at the other end of the line agreed that it was an exceptionally high quarterly bill, and he promised to look into it and write to her. Katie never understood the widespread criticisms of the nationalised industries; they always seemed to her civil and effective. She served a customer and took her coffee-break. Now the day seemed settled, she allowed herself the pleasure of ringing Andrew. She felt fear and excitement as the phone rang. His secretary answered.

"He's at a meeting all morning. Give me your name and number and he'll ring you back." Katie said who she was, he knew the number. He usually confirmed their dates. *He'll ring later.* She was sure, she told herself, that he would ring later. Slowly, the shop crept to the foreground of the day. Pam was to work Katie's late night tomorrow. Every time the phone rang she waited to be summoned to the desk; but it was never for her.

"Are you by any chance waiting for a call?" Pam noticed. "Is it the detective by any chance? I hope you don't mind my asking."

"No, it's someone else."

"Oh, I see. Are you going out tonight?"

"Yes, only for a drink and a meal with a couple of friends." *Another lie, without a moment's thought.* She vowed to make honesty a habit – in the future.

When, by four, he still had not rung, Katie, taking advantage of Angela's tea-break, used the phone again.

"He called and I gave him your message." There was nothing to say to the secretary. She walked back to her colleagues clustered around the table. There was no work to do. If he wanted to make it tomorrow instead, she would have to put Fred off. Her mother had always said that you should never cancel an appointment if something more exciting came up. She knew that her mother was right, but she knew that she would do it now – and not for the first time.

She was changed and waiting, unable to settle to any other activity. She had not gone to the pub in case he rang. She took a glass of wine, lit a cigarette and waited. It would be like Andrew to turn up with a busy excuse – after all, it was only half past seven. She looked at the clock for the tenth time. By half past eight his coming seemed less likely and an hour later extremely unlikely. She could have seen Fred, after all; she was in a restless bad mood. The cigarettes and wine had eaten her appetite. She wandered into the bedroom, took off her pearl necklace and hung it on the nail beside the mirror. She avoided looking at her reflection. From her jewel box she picked up the mass of mainly plastic trinkets held in a tangle of necklaces. She was looking for the tiny worn-leather ring box that had belonged to her grandmother. It was not there. She looked again. It certainly was not there. Next, she opened a metal box that sat on the chest of drawers. It was here she kept three old watches: her mother's gold one and two silver ones from her grandmother. The box was empty. Her past had disappeared. She rummaged through her underwear – years ago she had put her treasures there when she went on holiday. The knot of stretchy tights and hooked tangled bras hid nothing now. The polaroid camera was still in the bottom drawer. Only the ring and watches had gone. She rang the police to report the robbery.

Chapter eleven

Fred put the phone down, felt upset: stupid ass, he told himself. She had a life of her own, not hanging around waiting for him to come and rescue her like some bloody knight. He wondered what she was doing tonight. Why didn't she tell him? Why should she? He had to think about it. He was not too susceptible to women now, no – not that he was thick-skinned or cold. Once, once he had been fanatical . . . that had been Carol. He had really wanted to marry her. It was strange seeing her in Oxford Street a few months ago, the woman he thought he was going to die for, to kill for. She'd still looked quite good. Her figure had thickened a bit and her skin no longer had that sensitive glow he remembered. Now she was married to a supermarket manager in Tottenham and had two kids. He wondered, without much curiosity, if that had been the man he had found at her breakfast table when he turned up unexpectedly that morning. Now he could not be bothered to ask her, to offer her a moment's discomfort. That woman, Katie, had looked good – her face had shone out. He saw her as she had been sitting close to him on the sofa; he imagined her lying underneath him, he fucking her furiously, she looking all aglow. Come off it, he told himself, what's the point? She might not even go to bed with me. There was something a bit grand about her even though she only worked in a shop. She did not giggle girlishly, easily, like other women. She did not get all steamed up and a bit odd when they were close. It was more like having a friend. Again, he thought of her body, what it might look like, wondered what she was doing tonight. Anyway, he would see her tomorrow. He had just finished shaving when the telephone rang. It was the station, the Chief Superintendent CID, his boss.

"Something extremely sensitive and not at all pleasant, I wouldn't doubt. If you could go along to 143 Mount Street as soon as possible. The man there will fill you in on the details we have so far . . . Thank you, Anchor. Let me know what you think, as soon as you can."

Fred took time to make himself coffee; maybe it would be his last chance that morning. He dressed deliberately, choosing a dark suit, a serious striped shirt and dark-maroon tie. He felt clear-headed. Recently there had been too much trivia. This sounded more interesting.

Where Mayfair tapers away from commerce towards the green of Hyde Park, two steps up from the pavement stood a polished mahogany door with brass furnishings which was set into the pink terracotta façade of a substantial Victorian apartment block. The door, which ensured privacy to the residence of a senior Home Office civil servant, was opened by a young uniformed police officer.

"Police Constable Thomas, Sir." The young officer introduced himself and led Anchor into a large room at the rear. The walls were divided by pilasters in a marble that matched the fireplace. All was perfect order – rugs carefully placed on a parquet floor, Regency chairs and a sofa as well as a couple of small tables, on one of them a tray with decanters with silver tags at their necks and crystal glasses. He looked out of one of the three tall windows to a small walled garden below, ivy on the wall, a few tubs and a nude statue. Not an enthusiast's patio.

"There's this, Sir." Fred Anchor pulled the note out of the ragged envelope.

I am too ashamed to go on. I live in fear because I am being blackmailed and my funds are exhausted. Knowing I will be exposed I am finished.

Like an office memo the note was initialled at the bottom.

"It's downstairs, Sir. The housekeeper rang us. It's Sir Joseph Laskey, some nob at the Home Office."

"Who opened the letter?"

"The housekeeper. Sleeping tablets by the look of it, Sir."

"Has anyone contacted the doctor?" Anchor turned and gazed out of the window again.

"He's on his way, he's coming from Great Marlborough Street. They'll put him on first, he should be here within the hour."

The constable stood aside to allow his superior to pass. They both stepped inside the adjoining room, a bedroom: curtains drawn closed, bed made, nothing extraordinary – extremely ordinary, in fact.

"He's downstairs, Sir."

"Yes, I heard you the first time." He turned and descended the narrow staircase.

"Sorry, Sir."

"Does the housekeeper live here?"

"No, Sir. She comes in every day to do the cleaning, the shopping and to leave the old boy an evening meal. She's popped home now. She was overcome, crying, shock." Anchor looked at the constable's young eager face and smiled. "We told her to be back before ten, that you'd want a word with her." His voice had become more confident. "She hardly ever saw him, she said. The fact is, Sir, there's a room down here that's kept locked, she's never seen inside it. We haven't done anything about it; we were waiting for you, Sir. Probably nothing important." Then, after a pause, "I shouldn't think so, anyway."

"Really. We'll open the mystery box. Oh, I suppose you're too young to remember that programme."

"Sir?"

The door directly in front of the bottom of the stairs was locked. The doors to the other two rooms in the basement stood wide open. The room at the back was well-lit with the curtains drawn open. Fred entered and looked in the bed. The dead face was wrinkled into waxy folds of skin, the face of a man of about sixty, he guessed – fittish, but without his own teeth. He looked to the bedside table. There they were in a glass of pinkish liquid alongside a spy thriller, a telephone and a bottle of pills. He looked back to the face. The profile was framed in beige vomit. The collar of pale-blue pyjamas showed over the turned-down sheet. The bed was perfectly neat. The sign of a guiltless life?

In the bathroom, across the passage leading to the garden door, underwear was thrown in the corner. Now it need never be washed. A half-empty tumbler stood on a glass shelf beneath the mirror. He sniffed, expecting water, but inhaled gin. "Fingerprints, Thomas."

"Yes, Sir."

He peered into the mossy, moribund yard that served as a garden, before re-entering the bedroom. He searched the pockets of the grey pin-striped suit that hung over a valet stand. In one of those small jacket pockets that is concealed by a larger one he found a set of keys neatly held in a black leather case. From the dangling bunch he selected one which fitted the door facing the stairs. It turned easily. Inside was pitch black. He pushed a light switch and a small photographic darkroom was revealed, bathed in an orange glow. He exchanged the coloured bulb for one from the bedside lamp. A clothes line with plastic pegs on it was strung across the darkroom along the right-hand side. On a wooden trestle table were trays, empty and dry; next to them, large yellow envelopes. On the floor, under the table, stood chemicals for the photographic process in large brown bottles and plastic containers. He tilted one of the envelopes and allowed the black-and-white prints to slide out on to the table. They fanned out like playing cards.

It was a sequence. In the first, a small girl, naked, was sitting on the edge of a table. It did not look as if it was taken here, he thought, without certainty. A light on a stand was next to the table in the picture. The child's legs were apart, he could see it all clearly. Little girls are so definite, he realised, taking a deep breath. Next, a man stood beside the child, his old body girdled in rolls of fat, his hands were under his paunchy belly pointing his penis towards her. The little face stared anxiously at the camera, as if imploring them to finish. "Good God!" exclaimed Constable Thomas. Fred took out his pen and poked the pile around with it to view the final print. The child was looking towards her own shoulder as the sperm squirted over it. She was definitely not smiling. Anchor sighed, thrust his hands in his pockets and left the room. Thomas, who had pushed himself against the door-frame, to allow him to pass, stepped back inside to gaze at the prints.

Anchor dealt with the doctor, the fingerprint men and finally the housekeeper. He told her not to return; she would hear from them. He collected her keys.

The Chief Superintendent returned from lunch in time to hear a verbal report. His first words after hearing the story were: "It had to be the Home Office." They decided that inquiries should be made from the man's address book. Anchor was given the name of an officer who kept up to date with known paedophiles and with their corner of the porn market. Several times the Chief Superintendent told Anchor, "For God's sake, keep this discreet. It isn't going to do anyone any good." The Chief Inspector hoped that this was not altogether true.

The bed was empty when he returned to the Mayfair maisonette. Bedclothes lay rumpled on the floor. The stained pillow showed an impression of the dead man's skull. Tomorrow, more photographs – then listing and packaging what was needed. The wife – they were separated – lived in Malta, and the Consul would inform her this afternoon. He looked through the prints again. He fidgeted, anxious to get to the fat man. Who were the others involved?

He felt comfortless, indecent. Private disgusting innermost parts of other humans were to be put under scrutiny. Needing to go to the lavatory he was surprised to discover that he could not bear the thought of using this one. He left. There were interviews with the old horror's colleagues, paper, mounds of paper to be covered.

Although Katie could not see him tonight, he wanted to see her. To have his hand held, like a child, he thought, shaking his head. Should he phone her again? No. For a sociable drink he could find someone else.

Chapter twelve

If Andrew did not ring yesterday, all the more likely he would ring today. This reasoning cheered Katie. *And* she would say no: better still! Tonight she would see Fred.

She unscrewed the grinder lid. Evenly ground powder; the age of miracles had passed. She smelt the coffee and felt sick. She made tea. Should she have an egg? As the idea formed she turned to the sink and heaved out a thin stream of colourless liquid. She drank black tea. She was hungry, but with the thought of food came a taste and smell that her imagination turned to a sensation of vomit. Must be sickening for something, she thought. *Oh, how I hate flu.* Last night's indulgence had been modest, not enough to account for this. She went to work.

She felt sick all day and at the same time had an obsession with food. She actually felt much better immediately after the egg and chips at the cafe. It had been instant, seen and consumed without time for her imagination to process it. During the afternoon the nausea returned along with the desire for food. Sleep seemed the only alternative to this foul cycle. There was not sufficient business in the shop to distract her.

Angela announced, "I've got some bad news, I'm afraid. Alex has had a mild stroke. It must have been that carry-on with the thieves, I suppose. It was too much for him at his age."

"Well, this is it." Pam summed it up.

They all contributed to a get-well card which they all signed.

Once home, she rushed to her bed and closed her eyes. Her head whirled with remembered smells and appetites until, finally, she fell asleep. The doorbell woke her. There were two plainclothes policemen who asked if they could come up to talk to her. They had just sat down when the bell rang again. This time it was Fred.

"Listen, there are some policemen upstairs. Do you want to see them?"

"What's it about?" He looked surprised.

"It's just a minor robbery." He frowned. "I've had a few things pinched. Listen, why don't you go and wait in the pub, The Weymouth, on the corner." She pointed the direction. "It won't take long, then I'll come and join you. Sorry." She wanted to kiss him, but the moment passed. He was turning away.

He turned back towards her. "See you in a minute, then. Don't go fancying any of those coppers, they're rotten sorts you know!" He wanted to kiss her, but the moment passed. She turned, the door closed.

The policemen were seated, but on the alert, looking about the room. They started to rise. She signalled them back to their seats.

"I am Detective Chief Superintendent Boswell. I'm in charge of the case we've come to discuss. This is Detective Constable Adams. Miss Brown," he paused, looking directly at her, "Mrs Anselmo has given us your name as someone who knew that the family were staying in London. Now, I must emphasise that these inquiries are confidential. They are extremely delicate. *Any* disclosure could be very damaging." His look softened. "It is a measure of our regard for you that I say anything. This is secret and of great importance. Do you understand?"

Katie replied uncertainly that yes, she did understand.

"Now, Miss Brown, I think that you'll also understand we have to check on every possible lead, any small detail can help us at this stage."

"I'm sorry, I don't really understand. I thought you'd come about the robbery."

The policemen looked at each other. The younger of the two, who had not spoken yet, asked, "What robbery?"

"The things that are missing from my flat. I rang you about it last night."

"Who did you ring, love?" asked the older man.

She did not like the 'love', but let it pass. "Tottenham Court Road."

"I expect they'll see you about that soon. This, I fear, is a more serious matter. What do you know about the Anselmo family?"

"I don't even know who they are. I've never heard the name before."

Again the men exchanged a glance. "Tamara Anselmo?"

"Oh, Tamara. I didn't catch her surname. I met her once. She was here the other evening with a couple of friends of mine. Is she all right? What's this all about?"

"Nothing I tell you must go beyond these walls." He looked about him as if to explain walls, then back to her. She agreed, feeling like a nervous idiot. "Her cousin, a baby three weeks old, is missing. The baby has been kidnapped. A ransom note, posted in the West End, has been received by the family. You can appreciate that in matters like this we often keep the press out of it. I expect you've heard of similar cases?" She nodded. "Well, the press are co-operating with us this time. It can be the difference between life and death. That's how important it is that you keep everything said here secret."

"Of course I'll keep it secret, but I really don't see how I can help."

"Now, you say that you only met the young lady once. I want you to tell us everything about that meeting and anything else that you might think is relevant."

She paused for thought, then told them what Tamara and the others had said and done. They asked her if she knew the Anselmo family address in London. Only that it was in Highgate, as she had said. Boswell thanked her and, after a final warning about the secrecy of the affair, descended the stairs. Adams thanked her and hurried off after his boss.

She felt cheerless; things were not getting any better. The one warm spot – that Fred was waiting for her. She did her hair, put kohl in her eyes and left to join him.

"What are you having?"

"A beer, please. Half of bitter will do." Her throat was dry. She looked around the bar. There was no one she knew.

"How did they get in?"

"What, the police?"

"Listen, Katie. Are you all right? You look a bit pale."

"Ah, yes. I see what you mean. No, they didn't come about the robbery." Katie looked around; no one was listening. She spoke in a rapid whisper. "A baby's missing and I met her cousin on Saturday. The family is here in London because it's too dangerous in Sardinia. Now it's happened here. There's been a ransom note, so maybe they'll get the child back." He was about to speak but she continued to whisper close to his ear. "It's all secret. I only told you because you're a policeman. I shan't tell anyone else, of course."

"Don't you dare tell anyone else. I've heard about the case, but not about the note – it must have come in this evening. Kids, it makes me sick!" His face contorted with vehemence. "I've been put on something to do with child abuse. I've been dealing with it all day, in fact. I can't tell you about that, either. I shouldn't think you'd want to know, quite honestly." He looked drained by the words. She took his hand.

"I don't usually come into contact with trouble."

"Well, you're having your ration now." He gave her a sad smile.

She grinned briefly. "What I was going to say is that usually it's other people's troubles and I think, well, I'll listen, maybe offer help, it's never that much." He nodded and squeezed her hand. "I think really it has nothing to do with me and once they've left I'll get on with my silly old life. I've come to realise it isn't that simple: it affects you, saps something. Do you know what I mean?"

"I think you're right. I should be worried about it in my line of business." He said it lightly.

"Maybe you should be aware . . ." She laughed at the pretentious note that she had sounded.

"Listen, I have an idea. You don't have to agree. Let's go back to Maida Vale. I want to have a bath and a change."

"OK," said Katie dully.

"I can leave you with a drink. Then there's a goodish restaurant nearby where we can have a quiet meal. That is, unless you'd rather do something more exciting." He looked to her for a response. There was none. "Would you like to see a film?"

"I don't need to, life's developing into a sort of movie script. I could do with the peace."

He settled her on the brown leather chesterfield with a tumbler of gin and tonic.

"Turn the television on, if you want to," he yelled from the bathroom.

"No, thanks." With the drink and quiet she felt content for the first time that day. "I thought you lived in a semi, all fitted carpets and stereo, with a bar in the living room," she shouted.

"I don't understand . . . I don't know what you mean."

She had not thought of him as the kind of person who chatted from the bath. She found that pleasing. Also the obvious care, the taste with which he had decorated and furnished the place. Everything was new; it showed confidence, no pretence of a background.

He came in, his face pink. She wondered if his body was pocked and pasty. He took a drink, sank into the canvas chair and crossed his legs. He was wearing jeans, very clean and well pressed, shiny brown shoes, a tweed jacket and an open-necked red shirt.

"Are you hungry?"

"Starving!"

"Come on, then. I want to ask you a few questions. What's all this about your stuff missing . . . ?"

"I refuse to answer any questions until I've seen my lawyer."

"Come off it, mate," he assumed a thick London accent. "The way you're going you'll have all the police forces of the world after you."

"That's more like it. Anyway, I might enjoy that!" she added gleefully.

Before the end of the meal he had made a possible connection between the telephone bill and the robbery. She wanted to go on assuming the bill was a mistake. He suggested that the couple upstairs might be the culprits. There had been no break-in, so she found it hard to disagree totally. He found her notion that neighbours, even rogues, don't behave like that in their own backyard, laughably naive.

Back in his flat he made coffee and poured brandies. He had the correct glasses, she noted, even if he lacked the bar. By half past twelve they were lying on his bed, naked but for their pants. She found him lovely from the neck down. His skin was extraordinarily white, smooth and soft like liquid to touch. They stroked each other, gently kissed each other's face, neck and shoulders, their bodies rubbing, their feet caressing each other's legs. They moved, in silence, under the duvet and made love. It was strong and extraordinarily good, for both of them, especially for the first time. They fell asleep in each other's arms. Later, as Katie stirred she saw him awake, looking at her. Her hand went automatically to straighten her hair. He smiled. "Would you like me to drive you home now or in the morning?"

"Can I stay? I'm very sleepy."

"Good," he kissed her.

He was moving, coming on top of her. She looked at her watch: six thirty. She must go to the lavatory. It was not the main problem – the gnawing hunger and nausea had returned. She could not bear him touching her, it was hard to protest. After all it was her body, not mind, that was sick. She must still like him, she reasoned; but matter triumphed. She turned away and rolled off the low bed, not looking at him as she went.

She heaved, but nothing came up. Sitting on the closed lavatory she read an article in *Scientific American* about processing diesel fuel from oil. She was cold and tired, felt awful, but dreaded going back to bed. In the kitchen she found a Ryvita rusk and, nibbling on it, she crept back to the dim bedroom. His hands behind his head, he watched her. Rigid with cold, she picked up her sweater.

"Are you going to make me get up now? It's only seven. Why not come back to bed for half an hour? Is anything wrong?"

"I'm sorry, it's not you. I don't feel well. It's probably nervous dyspepsia. I don't want to make love."

"That's all right." He turned back a quarter of the bed and she lay down, icy cold, against the hard warm side of his body. Soon it was she who put her arm out and rolled over to cover him.

Chapter thirteen

"It's not busy, can you take your coffee-break with Lotte? You may as well go off now." Angela watched as Katie walked swiftly to the lift. Lotte went to the office. If she had not been allowed an early break Katie might have left anyway. She felt too tired and rotten to go on, like a puppet, performing her tasks. Passing the telephone room she looked in, from habit. Carol took her earphones off and joined her. The smell of coffee made her heave. She took tea and a bun. As Carol sat next to her she shuddered.

"Hey, Katie, are you all right?"

She told her friend about the sick–greed feelings.

"You're pregnant," Carol whispered into her ear.

"It's the bloody immaculate conception, then!" They giggled. *There I go again, telling the quick convenient lie*. She smoked one of Carol's cigarettes. It made her feel more sick, but smoking was a reflex reaction to any situation.

Vegetarian food was the only lunch that tempted her. The free meal last night justified the present expense.

The day dragged on until she was called to the telephone. It came as a sudden reminder of Andrew, but it was Gina, from Sardinia. Gina spoke rapidly, not directly about the kidnap, rather about its emotional impact. Italian emotion seemed to be more on tap, more acceptable. Katie's deep concern sounded maybe cool by comparison. The cashier was listening; and probably Carol upstairs as well. However, bound by secrecy, they avoided any exact details.

Ten minutes later and another call. *This must be Andrew*. The disappointment sounded in her voice when she heard it was Fred.

"No, I feel fine now ... Sorry, tonight's not possible. Listen, can I ring you on Saturday? I'm working ... You too, bad luck ... OK." The cashier, all attention, handed her paper and pen. She took down the number. "Thanks for last night ... Thanks for ringing ... See you soon."

"Angela, can I make a call, please?"

"As long as it's not Italy." She laughed; Katie smiled indulgently.

"Katie Brown? Oh, yes. You rang the other day. Andrew's out on location all day. I can leave him a message. Or else could you, please, try again on Monday?"

"Thank you." She felt shunned and numb. Angela and the cashier seemed to be both staring at her. She was conscious of awkward stilted movements, like a drunk trying too hard to appear sober.

It was not until she was half-way home, with movement and the fresh air that she sensed being back in the middle of her own body. The previous bad feelings seemed fair exchange for the joy of just being normal again. She wanted to walk and walk, not to arrive, never to go home again. She entered The Weymouth and slumped alongside Laurence who sat at the corner of the bar. *Strange to love the poisons that destroy us.* It would be stupid to say so, she realised, as they eagerly partook of nicotine and alcohol. Those deadly twins muffled the bad feelings lurking within.

She shrugged her shoulders as she told him about Andrew not calling. Trying to convince herself of its unimportance, she was still all in earnest when she asked if he thought Andrew was avoiding her. What should she do?

"Well, paranoia is usually inappropriate. I remember you told me that one. I always treasure those little homilies. That's not a bad one."

"Thank you." Her brevity was intended to encourage him to continue. Perhaps to irritate, he sipped his beer with slow deliberation. "Well, what do you advise as my expert on paranoia?" she prompted.

He gazed at his glass, lowering it to the table. "If you have an affair with a married man, there is nothing terribly wrong with that. I have done it myself."

"Well?" She gave a gentle jab with her elbow to prod him on.

"Well, it's just that he can't give you much, I don't only mean time. And if it turned out, like now, that all he's giving you is insecurity . . ." Katie shrugged her shoulders again, "so all you have is a fraction of an affair plus a lot of insecurity – then I think you should ask yourself why you want the relationship to continue at all." She waited thoughtfully. "One day, one or other of you had to tire of the cosy little fantasy. After all, it had nowhere to go, as far as I can judge."

She hoped that she would not forget these wise words but an overriding desire was saying: Ring Andrew again, ring him now, at home. She had once found the number in his diary and written it in her own. A secret never-to-be-used treasure.

By closing time she was too tired to eat, to do anything but go to bed. She was dimly aware that upstairs the baby was whining. The stamp of feet going down the stairs and the door banging shut roused her enough to look at the clock. It was only a quarter past twelve. She turned on the radio, which oozed moony ballads perfectly suited to her boozy emotional state. *What was it Noël Coward said about cheap music?* Melodies carried her in and out of consciousness. The cries from upstairs wound up to a piercing climax, transcending the radio. Those tiny lungs must break, or would his heart break first? She mused sentimentally.

Finally, in dressing-gown and slippers she crept up the smelly stairs, along the corridor towards the lighted rim of their door. She tapped. If anyone answered she was going to say, "I heard the baby crying and wondered if you wanted to ring the doctor." She knocked harder; the yelling was suspended for a few seconds, then resumed at the same pitch. The broken door swung from its upper hinge and was half-secured by a padlock and chain. Crawling through the gap she stayed on her hands and knees until, through the lobby, she was in the bigger room. Rising to her feet she whispered to herself, "The law should be upheld!"

The light from the front room shone dimly through the bedroom door, where the baby was hidden on the other side of the eiderdown pushed up against the rails of the cot.

As Katie leant over, the cries died away. Even in the soft dim light of the bedroom she could see a blotchy red and wrinkled face; there were no tears. This somehow made it worse. She lifted the baby from the cot and felt rapid deep pants against her chest. Hugging closely, she walked to the other room, swaying from side to side, cooing, whispering "shooey, shooey". She smiled: it was quite satisfying, flattering, as the calming effect became evident. She sat down beside the unlit fire, supporting the tiny body under the armpits, the head drooping forward to a natural angle of repose. The shoulders were lifted almost to the top of the head, from which, she noted, the dandruff seemed to have cleared.

She lowered her own head to look into the pink-rimmed eyes that stared darkly and uncertainly forward. The shadowed bags under the eyes were no longer to be seen. Were they only temporary? Was this the same baby? It did seem finer-featured, prettier. Absurd. She was drunk and tired. Babies defy the ordinary facial descriptions, but somehow she doubted that this was her old friend Brendan. "Brendan?" A myopic stare answered her. A half-full bottle of milk from the table was sucked quickly away, followed by gurgling noises emanating from the padded, plastic-covered bottom. She was not going to investigate. "I shouldn't really be here at all," she explained apologetically. "Now, listen to me – you're going back to your bed and to sleep. Do you understand?" With the small weight of the head on her shoulder she walked gently back to the bedroom . . . "shooey, shooey". She left the baby, face up with the eiderdown over its lower half. On the floor beside the bed was a screwed-up pink sweet wrapper. *The bastards: one of my Sardinian sweets. That proves they have been in my flat.*

She had just stretched out in her cool bed when the front door opened violently, rattling the pram. Afraid – she had so nearly been caught – she waited for the crash; instead, a noise like half a dozen unwilling cows being loaded into a truck was moving up the stairs. Only a foot from her, through the wall, the woman screamed, a slap sounded, then minutes of muffled struggles.

"Please, Al, I *do* care. It's not my fault." More struggles and whines. "I *do* care."

"Shut up, you stupid cow! Shut up!" The woman started to scream and was slapped. "Get up the fucking stairs!"

"Leave me alone, then." They crashed, shouted, wrestled their way up; the door clanked and banged.

Soon the awful descant of the baby's screams aroused more activity, louder shouting. Katie held her breath, listening. Recalling the sweet paper she felt no annoyance, even with herself, for not trying to aid the woman. Eventually, her interest drifted back to sleep. Her last word, 'Andrew'.

Chapter fourteen

In the dark at five in the morning Katie took a honey sandwich and a cup of tea back to bed. She also took her diary from the desk. A long way back 'P' was scrawled in the margin. She had forgotten to mark a period, she told herself and scanned the more recent entries, trying to remember, to make a connection: the towels, the tampons, buying the stuff, staining a sheet, an embarrassing moment. She found no clues. Wednesday after Wednesday, 'A' for Andrew. The memory felt like sunshine on her face. It was good, she knew, not only in retrospect. There was a particular Wednesday she remembered not putting her cap in, it was due so soon. There must, there must have been another. She searched frantically, but found no evidence. Then she felt very calm. The weeks had passed, the year rushed away. If this were true – she turned the pages, counting – she had missed three now. For the first time she did not panic. Instead of thoughts of money, getting it over as soon as possible, this time she wanted to wait. She sipped her tea. *Wait? What for?* She smiled at her own stupidity, not wanting to do a thing about it. Negative was the word that came to mind. The tea had a tang of olive oil about it, the bread tasted of onions. She could smell details even from upstairs – or was it some part of her own mind? She started to cry. "I want someone to smile on me," she shouted. And then inside herself, 'It's my secret, my own secret.'

The morning had an air of unreality about it, the important event lurked undone. She did not ring Andrew.

"You look a bit pale today, if you don't mind my saying so," said Pam. "Did you have a late night last night?"

"No, but the people who live upstairs kept me awake. It's difficult to get back to sleep."

"Oh, yes. I know. I had a period of not sleeping when I broke up with Bill last year. I told you about that, didn't I?" Katie looked straight at her, not sure. "Anyway I ended up taking pills. Maybe you've heard of them, Mogadons?"

"Yes, I've heard of them."

"They're very good. My mother takes them, actually, but I gave them up. I didn't want to be a slave to drugs." She looked about her. "You know, I hardly like to say this, but my mother takes pills to go to sleep and pills to wake up during the day. Do you think it's awful?"

"It isn't good." Katie was searching for sympathetic words when Lotte approached them. Pam quickly changed the subject.

"Have you fixed up your Christmas holiday yet?"

"Not really . . ." Katie's hesitant reply allowed Lotte to answer the question.

"I am saving money. I go to a friend's and she buys all the food. She is German also. We have company like this. I don't want a fuss."

"It's not much of a holiday, anyway, this year. They only give us what they have to." Pam further dampened the spirit of Christmas Future.

"That is so right." A customer came in and Lotte, with prissy little steps and hands clasped in front of her in obsequious piety, went to serve.

"Bill wants to go to a holiday camp. The one where

89

he used to work, on the security side. He has mates there." Katie smiled. "I don't fancy it that much really to tell the truth, but I don't want to stay at home. My parents – they won't have Bill in the house. I can't think of anything else we could afford. It's all very awkward at the moment. I expect you understand. Don't tell the others."

"Of course not. I expect I'll go to my sister's, as usual. The only trouble is that it's all very county and everyone else is married. I feel like the ugly sister at the ball."

"Oh, I'm sure that's not true."

"No, they're kind and generous." She wanted to redress the balance further. It just seemed impossible to contemplate going away with this all-pervading nausea.

Lotte came back. "I was wondering . . . well, I would like to ask Katie a favour, I'm sure you don't mind." Pam's eyes turned briefly up to the ceiling. She shook her head at Katie, who waited to hear the request. "The point is, I would like to change my lunch-time. I will tell you why – I want to go to the Citizens' Advice Bureau. If I go early, this is better, no?"

"OK, I'll change with you. What's your problem?"

Lotte's landlord had asked her to leave. She had previously arranged to move in with her German friend in the New Year, only now she was convinced that she could profit financially from the change. Pam and Katie both smiled. They enjoyed Lotte's grasping ways.

The changeover of lunch-times annoyed Angela. Her insecurity sensed conspiracy if the staff organised without her. A dose of bad feeling restored the balance and she allowed the swap of times.

It was grey, misty, drizzling but mild. Katie, in the

Soho market, soon had a full carrier of fruit. It was the only food that interested her. Was this a throwback to ape ancestry, she pondered, her instincts on the surface now that she was pregnant? If only she could hang upside down – monkey business – the sickness would subside. Thinking her thoughts, she headed back along Old Compton Street, past Sandra's coffee shop. There had been a time when she and Andrew had customarily taken coffee and croissants in this, the last of the old-fashioned coffee houses. Out of habit she looked inside. It *was* his back. Immediately, she wanted to go in. Instead, she stood outside, staring between shelves of cream cakes on the other side of the window. She stayed so long that when the girl opposite him stopped talking, drawn to look back at her, Katie moved on. The girl was young, in her early twenties, effortlessly classy-looking: a simple shirt, a maroon cravat, her longish hair held at one side with a slide. The type who wore sleeveless green anoraks and drove a French car to the country for weekends. The type who, in some unfathomable way, was quite straight-forward. Katie got on with girls like her, despite (or because of?) their complete lack of any morbid strain.

Strange coincidence. It has to mean something. It was something, she knew that. Something more than his work or his family . . . the girl's nervous response had been apparent.

All the inspiration about the food had gone. She felt like dumping the bag in a bin, but carried it back to the shop. Now something was clearer. She was further away from tears than she had been yesterday afternoon.

Lotte offered her an avocado – she, too, had gone through the market. Katie refused.

"Do you know why the rich look younger for longer than the rest of us?"

Katie said, "No, tell me."

91

"Because they eat avocados; they are the best food in the world."

"Well, you live and learn."

"You know, that is so true!"

At home, Katie lit the gas fire, took out her diary and noted the week's events and non-events. She went to the kitchen, felt hungry, felt awful. In the fridge an open tin of tuna faced her. She closed the door, turned to the sink and heaved. *Water. Oh, God!* Her hands over her eyes, she returned to the front room, sat and sobbed, the noise coming from her nose. There were no tears. Suddenly, she stopped – quiet, morbid, worthless. The sad sequence of thoughts was logical: *When death came would she not fight? How does it happen? What makes people into winos and tramps?* The diary open beside her, she lit a cigarette. In the space at the back reserved for notes, she wrote:

> *Listen, baby, you've got to learn that life isn't all serene waiting. It's drinking and smoking. The nicest people often want to destroy themselves. Well, that's what your mother thinks and it's important that you have a close relationship with your mother – there's no substitute for it – that is something generally agreed upon. It's all right if you rebel later, if you must continue that old tradition. Anyway, you'll surely feel bad if you influence me too much. I don't want to burden you with guilt, even intra-uterine guilt, but I don't wish you any harm – we've got to learn to live together. Let's hope that it's going to be easy. Love can't be all that bad, always. It's not fair, I never wanted to influence anyone and now I have no choice. I can't even drink myself silly without hurting you. We'll have to make a pact, I know I'm*

not perfect – I can't speak for you.

Katie felt better after writing the message to her baby. She ate bread and a banana effortlessly.

When the doorbell rang at half past nine she expected to see Laurence; instead, a huge uniformed policeman stood looking up at the front of the house.

"Are you Miss Brown? I thought you might be out, it being Saturday. I've called in connection with the reported robbery. Can I step inside and ask you a few questions?"

She showed him up and he accepted the offer of tea. He looked tempted to smile at the list of missing items, but his eyebrows rose – he was impressed by the telephone bill. Finally, he summarised the findings and put his pad in a bulging breast-pocket. "I think I've got it all down. Thank you for the tea." He rose and, putting his helmet on, looked about eight feet tall.

Alone, she realised she had been glad of the company, the interlude from herself.

She paused just inside the room, the door on to the landing wedged open, the tea tray in her hands. For once, she had not heard them coming down the stairs. She stopped to let Alan Remer pass but he had interrupted his descent and now stood looking down on her from the upper stair, a torn letter in his hand. Katherine stood behind him, not wanting to be observed, but Katie could see swollen eyes and the bruises.

"This is yours." She took the ripped letter.

"It was . . . that is, it got opened by mistake." The woman's shaky voice came over his shoulder.

He stepped down and Katie had to move backwards to allow him to pass. Katherine walked quietly back upstairs. Katie set off along the corridor with the tray, but he barred the way, staring at her.

"It was a mistake. I don't hold with people interfering in other people's business, right? In fact, I don't want you helping with the kid anymore. We ain't going out like before, so you needn't bother. All right?"

"Sure." He deserved a sterner reply. She was aware that she would regret her own cowardly politeness later, when the fear had worn off.

"Are you upstairs?" he yelled. More steps on the stairs. "Katherine don't need friends, see, because she's got her hands full with the kid." He spoke now with friendly confidence, then turned and ran down the stairs. The front door crashed closed. In the kitchen, her rage mounted. *Why not say about the robbery? How dare they pretend it was opened by mistake, my name was typed and clear on the envelope. What about the phone bill?*

Soon it was clear to Katie that the Remers now knew about the bill. The letter, from the assistant manager of telephone accounts, confirmed their conversation regarding the charge for dialled units in their last invoice. The meter and line had both been checked and found to be working correctly. The balance of nine hundred pounds and fifty-six pence was still outstanding and he would be grateful for prompt payment. Tranquilly, she now regarded this as a minor inconvenience. Maybe she had two hundred pounds in the bank. She could go to debtors' prison – anything rather than pay for what she had not used. Her sister and brother-in-law would never allow her to go to jail, so she believed, even if she had wanted to.

She still had the letter in her hand when she opened the door to Boswell. He asked to come up. With him was a woman detective and two uniformed policemen. Katie thought the woman's name was Grant; she missed the constables' names. The room was full of people.

"A policeman was here a minute ago." Once spoken, it seemed like nervous, cheap cheek.

"Was that about the robbery, Miss Brown?"

She was about to comment on his good memory, but checked a second silly remark. The front door banging and footsteps thudding up the house held them in silence for a while. The constables, holding their helmets, and the woman detective sat uncomfortable, upright on chairs. Boswell and Katie, perched on the sofa, faced each other.

"You are sure that you met Miss Anselmo only on that one occasion?"

"Yes, when she came with my friends from Sardinia."

"You haven't heard from any of them since?"

"No. Well, yes." He frowned. "Gina rang me the other day, when I was at work, mainly to see how I was."

"She rang you from Sardinia?"

"Yes."

"Is she in the habit of phoning you from Sardinia, just to see how you are? Are you going to tell me that she didn't mention this case at all?"

"She used to," Katie was on the defensive, "ring me just to chat, but she hasn't done that for a long time, until the other day. She's extravagant on the phone." She shrugged her shoulders. "She can afford to be. I could hear that she was worried. She was sad, of course – so was I; but, honestly, we didn't say anything definite about it all. Would you like some tea?" She tried to ease the tension. Boswell brusquely declined.

"Do you know her number in Sardinia?"

"Yes, it's in my book." She moved to fetch her bag but Boswell put out his hand, making further effort unnecessary.

"Brian Carstairs. Do you know Brian Carstairs?"

She thought for a moment. *I know my memory's*

going. She thought again. "No, I don't. I've never known anyone of that name. Who is he?"

He persisted, ignoring the question. "Are you sure that you have never known anyone called Brian? You might not have known his surname. Brian anything?"

"I'm pretty sure that no Brian has ever crossed my path." She spoke deliberately. His assiduity was irritating. "Who is he?"

"He works for the Anselmo family, here in London. Think about whether you might have met a man called Brian, or even a man you've met recently who might not have told you his name, or told you an assumed name." His tone had softened.

"Try and think if you've told anyone about Miss Anselmo." She shook her head emphatically. "Would you mind if we looked around? We'll try not to disturb anything." The two constables placed their helmets on the floor and rose to their feet. "You've got a lot of books, you must read a lot." He actually smiled.

He's trying to win me round. In the films I would ask to see his search warrant. "No, help yourselves." She sat back, trying to feel comfortable. At a meaningful gesture from their superior the two men set off, in opposite directions, hesitated and then both headed for the bedroom. The door was too narrow for both to pass. After a second's silent confusion, one followed the other into the already lit room. She heard the wardrobe doors being opened, the hangers rattling, the drawers as usual sticking, and those under the bed thumping to the floor. Boswell saw her attention and, like a dentist, wanted to take her mind off the present. He cleared his throat, looked about for a subject and saw the desk. "This is a lovely piece of furniture. I expect it's been around for a year or two."

"Yes, it's Queen Anne."

"Do you mind?" She shook her head. He went over

and opened the flap, using the key as a handle. She wondered if he would see the diary with the writing about the baby in it. He closed the lid almost immediately.

"Have you read them all?" He peered at the rows of books, then behind them. The two emerged from the bedroom. One shook his head at Boswell.

"Are there other rooms, Miss Brown?"

She showed them to the kitchen and left as there was no room otherwise for two men to manoeuvre.

They were back in five minutes. They picked their helmets up from the floor in unison. "It's bit of a squeeze, the shower and the kitchen out there." The policeman was grinning at her. She wondered if he had needed to inspect the bucket of dirty underwear. Would that account for the smile? Boswell said he would see them back at the station and they left.

"By the way, there may be a call here for me, I gave the board your number. Now, I'm afraid, we have to go over it all again. I will have asked you some of these questions before. I can only assure you that it is necessary." Katie nodded, resigned. "Do you know Highgate at all?"

"Hardly. I've been to the cemetery once or twice for walks. I think most of it is closed now. I once had a Chinese meal somewhere in the village; maybe a drink on a summer's day. Really, that's about it."

"When were you last in Sardinia?"

She consulted an old diary, found the exact dates of the holiday of two years ago and he wrote them down.

"Now, when you were there did you meet any of the Anselmo family?"

"Gosh. I must have met half . . . maybe a dozen friends of Gina and Colette. I feel sure, though, that I would have remembered if I had met Tamara." She looked at her diary. "There was a French architect and his daughter, an Italian singer, three English people who live there, the actress . . ." he nodded in recognition at the name. "There were others, a few, but I don't remember names, just meetings, quick drinks. I'm not so very good at names."

"Think about it later, maybe something will come to mind." She pulled a disbelieving face.

"I have thought about it all, and I don't honestly think that I can help you very much . . . I'm . . ." The phone rang, Boswell picked it up. "Yes, who's calling? . . . Can you give me your name, please? It's for you. Laurence."

"Who the hell is that?" He was often jealous of her friends and so his angry tone was no surprise to Katie.

"The police are here at the moment. Can I ring you back later?"

"I only wanted to know if you'd come out for a drink."

"Maybe later. I'll ring you back or see you there. Bye. Sorry."

Boswell glanced at his watch, "Was that your boyfriend?"

She shook her head, wanting to say she was too old for boys. "No, just a friend wanting to know if I'd pop out for a drink. By the way, he brought me some cider from Devon yesterday, would you like a glass?" Both the woman detective and Boswell accepted, none of the 'not on duty' patter.

As she poured from the plastic container, her thoughts strayed. *I was drunk. I'm the connection but I'm not involved. How can the babies, the couple and the Sardinians be linked except by me?*

Boswell delivered a short lecture on secrecy, between sips.

The woman detective, still buttoned into her sheep-skin coat, wore grey tights that showed between the brown cloth of her skirt and her brown boots as she sat cross-legged at the table. Katie watched her drink. Maybe it strengthened her because now she spoke for the first time.

"Do you have a boyfriend?"

"No." She replied in the same fake, off-hand way that the questioner had used.

"Have you ever been married?"

Katie felt her hackles rise a mite. "No." She correctly guessed the next question.

"Have you ever had any children? Or lost a child, had an abortion, maybe?"

The neurotic spinster angle she resented, and answered no to every point. *Was it a mistake? This is not a game, the old reflex of lying won't stand up long. Maybe they will bother to find out, see the lies, the pretended instability that ensured abortions. It is all on medical records.* Her mind whirling for the instant, she was tempted to truthfulness, to forsake the good impression. She said no more on the subject, but put words to her earlier doubt. "There is something . . ." – Boswell sat forward – ". . . about the robbery . . ." He eased back again. *He thinks I'm wet, maybe a bit mad. At least I am trying to be truthful.*

"What about the robbery, Miss Brown?"

"Well, I think there may be a possible connection between the people who live upstairs and my things going missing and the phone bill."

"Didn't you tell the other police about this?"

"Yes, about the robbery, but this is to do with their baby." He sat forward again. "Sometimes, I babysit for them . . . well, I used to. They were out the other night, last night, actually, and although they hadn't asked me to I went up because the baby was crying all the time." She needed his approval, somehow, to continue. He nodded. "I thought the baby had changed.

What I mean is, it was a different baby." He was on the edge of the seat. "It's difficult to be sure. I don't see how they can have any connection with this."

"You say they live above? On the next floor? What's their name?" He wrote it all down on a scrap of paper, stood and put it in his jacket pocket. "We'll go and see, shall we?"

"Please don't bring me into it. I have to live here."

"I may have to involve you, but don't worry, they won't know that you sent us, not tonight." He turned to his colleague. "We'll go and ring their bell, shall we? See if there's anything in this. You stay put, young lady. We'll see you afterwards." He bent in front of her and swung his coat off the sofa, on to his arm. His companion pulled the collar of her coat about her ears as she went through the doorway. Having allowed her to pass, the Detective Chief Superintendent closed the door, and followed the woman detective down the stairs to the street.

Katie straightened her back and shuddered. The bell upstairs rattled. Thumping steps came down, two or three at a time.

"What's this all about? You've got no right to come into people's places without saying what it's about."

Steady steps climbed on up to the floor above.

She was washing the glasses, her hands trembling in the suds, when Detective Sergeant Grant opened the kitchen door and asked Katie if she would come upstairs. Once upstairs, Boswell gave no sign of recognition as Katie entered.

"We are the police. This is an important matter and we must ask for your co-operation. You live on the floor below? Yes? I must ask you if you can identify this child."

Katherine was holding Brendan wrapped in a shawl.

"That's Brendan, Mr and Mrs Remer's son. I know

him quite well." Should she ask a question? Play act? No, she did not want to seem slick, untrustworthy.

"Thank you. Miss . . .?"

"Brown, Katherine Brown."

"As I said, I'm sorry to have disturbed you – to have disturbed you all." He looked around at their faces. "It is important. I hope you understand."

"I don't bloody understand. You come in here without a warrant. Police, so you say. How do I know you're not lying?" Remer shook his fist at Boswell. Katie turned to go, she had a sneaking sympathy with him. "You're going to be in the shit for this. I'll write to my MP. It's not a fucking police state, you know. You can't treat us like this." Once in her room she lit a cigarette, then she heard them coming down. "Go on! Good riddance! Fucking cunts! Next time you won't get past the door, do you hear?" Boswell over-politely thanked him for his help. "You're bastards!" The door slammed. Five minutes later Katie's bell rang and she led the detectives back into her room.

"Was that the truth, about the baby? What you said upstairs?"

"Yes, that was certainly Brendan, it was their baby all right."

"Are you sure about what you told us previously?"

"I wouldn't have said it if I wasn't fairly sure."

"What do you mean 'fairly sure'?"

"Well, I was very tired." She had to stop herself laughing at the old euphemism.

"Are you sure, or only fairly sure, about the baby this evening?" He was irritated.

"I told you, I'm sure it's Brendan."

"Yes, well, we saw the birth certificate and some photographs, it seems to be correct."

"I'm sorry. I suppose it could have been a mistake. Maybe I was confusing the robbery and the kidnapping in some way. Maybe I'm more upset about it all than I realise."

He was watching her curiously. She lit another cigarette. "Try and take it easy," he said. "Here's my number, day and night. Don't hesitate to ring, even for something that may seem trivial." He shook her hand. Grant came over and did the same.

Afterwards, she rang Laurence. He said he would come over because, by now, at half past eleven, it was too late for the pub. She paced about waiting, thinking. They seem decent enough folk, but it's part of their job to get people to come along quietly. She was right not to trust them with personal information. She had already made herself appear unstable. Anyway, her private life was irrelevant – unless, of course, they fabricated some story. It was possible. She rubbed her cheek. When Laurence arrived she cried, said she was ill, which was true. He ignored her and drank in silence. She said she was going to bed. He told her to ring him in the morning if she wanted anything, if she was still ill.

Lying on her side in the dark she sensed her feelings going into eclipse, shutting off, gently slipping away. She would die if the trance continued. Downward drifting, further and further, she summoned sufficient will. The strength of her body returned until she could safely relax and sleep.

Chapter fifteen

"I want to see you, you miserable old bitch. Are you afraid to open up?" He was banging on the bedroom door with both fists. She clung to her duvet, wondering how long the door-panels could take it.

"What do you want?" She wanted to defuse the anger with words, her terror was seeing him.

"Come and open the fucking door." She saw the handle turn, he was pushing hard from the other side.

"What do you want to talk to me about?"

"Come and open the door."

"I'm in bed. It's Sunday morning. I'll see you later."

"That's about all you're good for – bed. We thought you were on the game with all those men here all the time. You must be nearly past it, wouldn't you say? You're just a frustrated old slag."

"If I'm so awful, why do you want to talk to me?"

"You think you're so clever. You can look down your nose at us, Mrs Shop Assistant Slag. You're wrong every time."

She slid out of bed, pulled on a pair of trousers, not risking the noise of an opening drawer to get at her underwear. She pushed her feet into her slippers and covered her naked top with a Shetland sweater. Outside she heard shuffling sounds. She crept into the front room, up to the door. The handle was moving back and forth, then it stopped; she put her ear to the door. She thought she heard him climbing the stairs, like a mouse. After a pause she turned the key silently, opened the door the merest crack to peer along the dark empty corridor. Her fingers stiff with tension, she slid the key from the inside to the outside of the key-hole, turned the key and hurried on tip-toe out of the house, leaving the front door open behind her.

"Jesus Christ, it's you, Katie. What the fuck are you doing here at this hour? Do you realise it's eight o'clock and Sunday morning?"

Tears poured down her face. "I'm so glad you're in," she sniffed. "Oh, Laurence!"

"Katie, this is like a soap opera. What's up? Are you ill again? Oh, God, I'm frozen! Come on up."

His legs were so thin and the fuzz of brown hairs gave them a greyish hue. He hopped up the stairs. The cold lino obviously hurt his bare feet. Not-quite-white pants bounced where they bagged at the seat. He wore a huge ribbed sweater above.

"I thought you had a smart dressing-gown – that tartan one the American bought you at Blooming-dale's?"

"I lost it."

"How can you lose a dressing-gown?" She was laughing while wiping away the tears.

"Have you gone kinky about men's wear? I suppose you think it's a good joke, at a loss for a prank, feeling sorry for yourself this dull Sunday morning, you decide . . ."

"I've just been *threatened*. I can't go back with that man in the house."

"Is it the wild Scot, come to humiliate?"

"It's nothing to do with Andrew, if that's who you mean. It's the yob from upstairs. He was pounding on my doors."

"What did he want?"

"He said he wanted to talk to me."

Laurence was filling the electric kettle, looking fed up. "So why didn't you talk to the man?"

"He was hammering at the doors, both of them. I was frightened. And he insulted me, he said disgusting things. I'm not exaggerating, honestly." Laurence sighed, nodded and plugged the kettle in before pushing several dirty cups and plates to the centre of the table to make room for his elbows as he sat opposite her.

They sipped coffee from large dark-green French cups. She told him what the man had said.

"Why is he so against you? I thought you helped them. What's gone wrong? There must be some reason, or is he plain psychopathic mad? Shall I ring the police?"

"I know what it is. It's to do with the police already. Well, I only know a bit what it may be, but I can't tell you."

"Well, thanks very much." He took up his cup.

"You will, as soon as I can tell you. That is, when I understand it myself."

"I was right first time – a soap opera. Listen, Katie, you've forgotten your script. I'm the one with problems tearing my hair out and crying."

"I can't go back there. And this should have been a lovely weekend." Tears again rolled down her cheeks. "I've got tomorrow off, two days running."

She persuaded him to go to Highgate for a walk. In the village he talked about architecture. In the cemetery she wept, yet again. In the gloom of a huge 1930s pub, over Bloody Marys, he asked her why she was so confirmed in her misery. He could not understand the impossibility of her telling.

For lunch they had pizzas in Soho. The afternoon was spent with the Sunday papers as near as safely possible to Laurence's two-bar electric fire.

The street was silent and empty, plastic rubbish bags sagged against the sides of doors, their bulges high-lighted by the street lamps. "Will you come with me to my flat? I want to collect a few things. Can I keep the shoes and anorak?"

"No, you can't. Come on, then, let's go."

A hold-all bag in her hand, she was glad to be safely outside again. It was warmer, more friendly in the street than in her flat now. They had just gone back across the road when a police car screeched around the corner and stopped outside Katie's flat. Boswell got out, so Katie handed her bag to Laurence and went over to him.

"Let's go inside, Miss Brown," No greeting, no handshakes. Reluctantly, she paced up the stairs. The floorboards creaked as the fire warmed the air. He told her to sit down. He remained standing in the centre of the room.

"Have you anything to tell us?"

"Only what you already know."

"Where were you going just now?"

"To stay with my friend Laurence, across the road."

The woman detective and the two constables came in and stayed by the door. Boswell went to the window.

"Did you see the man?"

"Yes, Sir. She was going to spend the night with him. They've been together all day, he says. We had a look inside that hold-all."

Boswell thanked the constable. They all looked at Katie. She went to get up, to go to the window, but Boswell shook his head. Afraid and angry, she spoke in a fierce staccato.

"I woke up and I was afraid. The man upstairs was outside my door insulting me. When he went away, I went across to see Laurence." She closed her eyes and

106

took a deep breath. "Laurence is a good friend of mine. He made me coffee, then we went for a walk and had a drink" – a pause – "in Highgate."

"Really? Do go on."

She would have liked to get back at him for making such an insinuation, but there seemed no point.

"I wanted to go out for a walk. He didn't want to. Then we went to the Portofino, in Old Compton Street, and had pizzas. We read the papers in Laurence's flat, then I came over here to collect a few things for the night. He came with me – like I said, I was afraid."

"Why didn't you ring me?"

"I don't know, honestly. It didn't seem to be connected . . . I don't know."

"Next time you don't know you had better let me decide. It was Alan Remer who frightened you?" She nodded. "Tell me what happened." She told him, not looking at him as she quoted the insults. "Do you happen to know where Mr Remer is now?"

"I've no idea."

Boswell walked to the door, his colleagues parted to let him through. He went downstairs to ring the Remers' doorbell. No one said a word. He returned to Katie's landing, signalled, and then followed the others up the stairs. Katie heard only faint murmurings, even though she stood in the doorway. When she heard them returning, she hurried quietly back to the sofa.

"His wife says he's gone to see his mother and may not be back tonight."

"Then I can stay here?"

"I think you'd better. If there's any trouble, phone us. We'll certainly be back to see you all – soon. Goodnight, Miss Brown. We can see ourselves out. I'll tell your friend to bring your bag up to you, shall I?"

She noted the subtle innuendo when he said 'friend'. He had sullied a good many words.

Chapter sixteen

A pattern was emerging, days tired, nights thinking –
not sleeping. It took a while to realise that the phone
was ringing. It sounded friendly once the ringing
became clear.

"You don't sound half-asleep, you sound half-dead
this morning. Are you all right?"

"Yes, I suppose so. To be fair, I don't know how my
voice is going to sound, first thing in the morning. Do
you always ring your friends at this hour?"

He remembered that early-morning call so many
years before . . . "Oh, no. Only my best friends."

"Well, it's a strange way of showing affection. How
are you? When am I going to see you? I think you're the
only policeman I really do want to see. They call every
evening now."

"It sounds as if they're giving you a bad time. If it's
all right with you, I'll drop by around half past six this
evening."

"That's fine. Oh, wait a minute. They'll probably be
here, the men in blue."

"I've thought of that. If they are there, only pull one
blind down; when they've gone, let them both down. If
they haven't called yet, leave them both up."

"What will you do then?"

"I'll ring you. It's only to avoid any embarrassment.
I'll see you later. Take care, now."

"It's my day off today. I'll try and be in a better

mood by this evening. I seem to have lost my sense of humour. See you then."

He said 'drop by' as if he wasn't staying – funny. She shrugged her shoulders. Returning to bed with a cup of tea and the Boston Women's Health Book she found the section on pregnancy, skipped the sisterly-feeling bit, and started on 'Taking Care of Your Physical Needs', subsection (a): Nutrition.

> Every day you must . . . [*must, indeed!*] (a) one quart (four glasses) of milk (equivalents such as cottage cheese and yoghurt are fine; skim milk is also good); (b) two eggs; (c) one or two servings of fish, liver, chicken, lean beef, lamb, pork or cheese (alternatives are dried beans, peas or nuts); (d) one or two servings of fresh green leafy vegetables – mustard, collard, or turnip greens, spinach, lettuce, or cabbage or fresh frozen vegetables; (e) two or three slices of whole-wheat bread; (f) a piece of citrus fruit or glass of lemon, lime, orange, or grapefruit juice; and (g) one pat of margarine, vitamin enriched. Also [*what, more?!*] (a) four times a week, a yellow or orange-coloured vegetable; (b) liver once a week; and (c) a baked potato three times a week.

There had never been a week in her life when she had eaten as much as the daily recommended ration! Every item on the list made her feel sick. Nothing was going to induce her to eat liver. Could it be true that every mother of a healthy child had stuffed that much down herself for nine months? Katie decided it was for fad-diet-orientated North Americans. She closed the book and dozed.

The list of local doctors in the post office showed more

deletions than entries. It would be a good start to a documentary on inner-city decline, she thought, imaging the next shot – a crowded, run-down surgery. The imagined scenario turned out to be accurate. Propped against the dark-beige wall of a waiting room, she waited for her name to be called. Doctor Hailey was a thick-set, middle-aged man. He gave her half a glance then looked down to his hand, which held a pen poised above a pad of headed paper. His desk-top was the only bright spot in the gloomy room.

"I'm pregnant and I want a letter to the hospital, the Central London."

"Are you sure you're pregnant?"

"Yes."

"You're not married, are you? Are you sure that you want this child?"

"Yes . . . I think so."

"Only 'think so'?" He glanced up.

"Yes, I do."

He wrote a couple of lines on his pad, tore off the sheet, scrawled on an envelope and then, with tender loving care, folded the letter, slipped it in and licked the flap. He was on his feet as he handed it across the desk. He passed her and was at the door calling for the next patient before she was out of the room.

As soon as she was home the carefully sealed envelope was steamed open. Addressed to the Obstetrics Department of the Central London Hospital, it read:

Katrina Brown
This patient thinks she is pregnant, suggest examination.

Satisfied, she made tea with the ready boiling water before, overcome by weariness, she took a nap. It was what she longed to do through all those endless days at work.

Two hours later and embarked on her usual route, she stopped at a nearer shop – Liberty's. She bought more fabric for the cushions, in case they discontinued those designs. The transaction did not take long but seemed agonisingly slow; her legs tight together, she waited for the bill and longed to pee. She descended the steps to the public lavatory at the back of the shop, on the corner of Carnaby Street, opposite Great Marlborough Street Magistrates' Court. Restored to a state of grace she went back into Liberty's and looked through the sweaters, soon finding the very thing. Only the price was wrong. She remembered the telephone bill, sighed – and signed a cheque. Swinging a bag in each hand she made her way home.

Hair washed, the new sweater covering the tight fit of her trousers, she could smell the freshness of the new cushion fabric inviting her to start work on it. Instead, she dithered about, agitated, until it was nearly six o'clock. She tore the pages of notes from her diary, where she had written to her unborn baby, and thrust them deep in the kitchen garbage. By habit, she went to lower the blinds before remembering not to. She turned away from her own blurred reflection on the glass and the first tears of the day flowed down her cheeks.

The tears continued, but behind the release she was calm, curious that so much weeping was possible: customarily, her misery used to wear itself out. Would the loss of salty water change her physically, chemically? She yearned for Andrew . . . If he came now, hugged her, told her they could be together, she would be cured . . . She sat up straighter – she would give up thoughts about Andrew. After all, what was there to lose? Nothing. Fred was reality, a calm embodiment of my desires, she told herself. He's not aggressive, chauvinistic, not a bad man.

It seemed luke-warm, though: love by default. A

common experience – I'll take it. Then she recognised that it was the warm expectation of laughter that was missing with him. Yet the other was just a bad habit, she thought in disgust. Being without Andrew will soon be no worse than missing a favourite radio programme. She would be lucky to have Fred; she determined to make it work, to love him.

In the kitchen she chewed a lump of wholemeal bread with a sprig of parsley. Carrying a glass of milk she went back to the main room. Movement made a comforting rhythm . . . *Eat well, sleep well, my darling child. Ignore the turmoil of your parent. It's only the façade, crumbling because it was no longer real. A new reality will form, be patient with me.* She leapt with terror at the suddenness of the bell. 'I won't answer it,' she thought. 'I'm afraid, I'm afraid. The old fears were gentle and long term.' She smiled at those final words, wondering how to reinterpret them.

As usual Boswell asked her what she had done during the day. "The doctor's, bronchitis," she said, then lit a cigarette. *Is there a psychology course for policemen that teaches that suspects light a cigarette after lying?* She went and let one blind down. Was Boswell waiting for the second to be lowered? The signal seemed blatantly obvious.

"I went shopping at Liberty's." She pointed to the package on the table, then pulled the front of her sweater out. "I bought this, too." No comment, she let go of the grey ribbed wool. She turned to the woman, Grant, serious in her sheepskin, at the table, and then looked back at Boswell whose head was bent in contemplation of the rug. He wore conventional clothes; ordinary haircut, grey streaks amid the dark brown; a firm face, not handsome but not ugly. Was he clever or just determined? Boswell was a great name. She wanted to speak to him, to establish a point of contact. Was it possible that this man shared any of his early namesake's ways? Was a sceptic? A tireless, grubby man of pleasure? No, this cold, hard man was not going to help her. No one could help her. *When you think that – you really need help!* She waited to see his face, to convince him to kindness. Finally, he looked up and spoke the words that ended any such hope.

"The Anselmo baby is dead. Its body was found this evening in the public toilet in Great Marlborough Street."

Katie closed her eyes, red–grey sparkling shapes whirled about. When she opened them, colour had left the room; it was all grey. She lurched from her seat – Grant went to grab her arm but missed. Rushing into the kitchen, she choked whitish-grey sick into the sink. When she turned, through eyes full of tears, she saw the blurred shapes of the detectives standing in the kitchen doorway. She wiped her face, rinsed the sink, took a glass of water and returned to the other room. For a while they sat in silence.

"You don't have a television, do you? It will be on the news tonight. The secrecy is over. We have appealed to the public for help. Are you sure you can't help us now?"

She lit a cigarette and shook her head, unable to speak.

"Well, we'll go – for the time being. You've got my number." They left in silence.

Five minutes after she had let the second blind down, the doorbell rang. Fred Anchor stepped quickly inside. They hurried up the stairs, he closed the door, took her arm and sat her on the sofa, next to him.

"Listen, Katie, I know what's happened and I know that you have nothing to do with it, but I really think that it's better if we don't meet again – just for a while." His eyes moved to look at her, and then away.

"Do you really mean that? You're not going to see me . . .?"

He clasped his hands and concentrated on them while he spoke. "I know this sounds harsh, but you have to believe me – I know about these things, more than you do." He was shaking his head. "It will only be for a little while. I haven't changed." She snorted in disgust. "I mean it, don't let it hurt us. It can't do us any good to be together at the moment. Do you understand?" Now he watched her, waiting.

"I think I understand quite well enough! I thought you were my friend. Oh, I don't care. I don't care about your precious career and I don't care if I see you or not." Now she wanted to cry, but felt rigid and dry. "I decided to love you," she spat the words out with hate, then saw the colour rising in his cheeks.

"I care a hell of a lot about you," he said with determination. Then, in a soft tone, "You must know that." He put his arm around her. She saw the white, manicured hand on the shoulder of her new sweater, felt the warmth of it, then the tears swelled out, down her still, pale face. She remained, her head turned away from him.

He kissed her neck. "Oh, Katie, I'm so sorry." He kissed her again and again until she turned and, without a word, stood up and led him to the bedroom.

They stripped. She pulled him on top of her. With hardly a glance and still in silence she demanded more, deeper, harder. The more it hurt, the better it felt.

"Don't come." She lay still, scowling.

"I can't – I've got to come." As he made his final thrusts she clung to him, intensifying the actions, enjoying the frenzy until, glad that he looked regretful to be done, she released him. It had been an exorcism. She rose and dressed, leaving him exposed on the bed. Glancing at him there, she despised what she saw –

white, damp and limp. She was brushing her hair as he dressed in sad, puzzled silence and then, crossing the room, he came to kiss her softly on the top of her head. "I'll ring you soon." She shrugged her shoulders.

When Katie was certain that he had gone she came out into the front room. Her foot knocked and broke one of the glasses and she kicked at the ruin, stamped on the pieces in rage. She walked down the street to The Weymouth but, instead of going in, walked around the blocks, one after the other, the wind and drizzle invigorating her. Back outside the pub, two lovers kissed as Katie passed by. She heard the woman mutter, "This is one way of doing it." It occurred to Katie that winter was the most romantic season. What did it mean, 'one way of doing it'? Silly intense things, the murmurings of lovers. She wondered if she envied them, and found she did – a little.

She could think of nothing else to do and so, fully awake and with the light on, she went to bed. She might get up again, the biological clocks had stopped, day and night relayed no signals. A little murder, the tiny corpse curled like a foetus, only partly visible in a lavatory bowl; she saw it as form and colour, with no more intensity than she could give to viewing many works of art. With her hands on her tummy she spoke.

"Listen. I don't know you, that should help. I always failed when love was a duty, like with my mother, or living with Peter . . . and now the two of us can hardly live apart, not right now. I can't imagine you, really, that's why the conversations are so one-sided. Are you listening? I'm talking to myself. I'm the little one: it's me the tiny, pitiful speck somewhere in me where these words are echoing about. I am trying."

The door burst open. Alan Remer stood next to the

bed. "Talking to yourself! You've got it coming to you, you miserable old bag. No one's going to help you!" He left, slamming both doors.

She sat rigid on her bed, listening to the racket from upstairs. It sounded as if they were smashing everything, screaming non-stop. Let it go on and on, she thought, let them come down here and smash all this – I want to be part of it. Then she stood up, locked the door, saw that it was nearly three o'clock, turned the light off and returned to bed. She lay in a trance, wondering which was the good or which was the bad – things happening or things not happening? From outside in the street came the sound of a car door being slammed loudly. She sat bolt upright in bed, trembling all over.

Chapter seventeen

Usually Angela did not sit down, she set the example – was always on the look-out for jobs. This Tuesday morning was an exception. After the morning's tidy-up she joined the rest of the staff around the table. Katie saw that Angela's pink, unlined face kept softening to a smile, and she felt she was addressing an alien.

"You're cheerful this morning, Angela. Have you won the Premium Bonds?"

Angela was pleased and blushing. "No, I wish I had, I could do with the money. Actually, as it happens, I met a very nice young man last night. I'm going to see him again at the weekend." The joy was evident.

Katie was pleased – at last, Angela had a man. For months now Angela's social, disco-going life had been disrupted by one girl friend after another abandoning her for a steady boyfriend. Pam expressed common-sensical delight and started to ask Angela questions. The two of them were the same age and similar in many ways – both on course, or hoped to be: jollity, romance and marriage. A simple tale. Only now, so late, too late, had Katie come to see any sense in this well-worn scheme. She had had her ration of passion but never settled well to sharing domesticity, the boring bits – the bread of the sandwich. How was it, Katie wondered, that these young things in particular – and, indeed, most people in general – understood the rightness of the old ways when it had taken decades for them to infiltrate her own sluggish mind? *What a mess. My mother always said that I would only learn the hard way.*

"By the way," Pam interrupted her musings, "have you seen that detective? I hope you don't mind my asking."

"Well, I did have a drink with him the other evening." She pursed her lips so that the corners drooped, and shrugged her shoulders in dismissal.

"Oh, I see. It's like that, nothing much. What a shame. Haven't you ever wanted to get married, Katie? Well, you're still a very attractive woman. You still could, of course."

Katie smiled. "No. I don't want marriage and never have."

The answer may have satisfied Pam but it made Katie query the truth of it. If it were lies, she was lying to herself these days. Yet would she marry Fred? No. And Andrew? Probably not. Being your own person was simple but sad.

Philosophy was replaced by sharp nausea. Also, she needed to pee. The intention to ask Pam to exchange coffee-breaks was frustrated by a summons to the telephone. Andrew came on the line to ask if they could meet the next day; she had many good reasons to reply that she would ring him back later.

During her break she left the shop so that the telephone conversation was protected by the privacy of the call box behind Jaeger's. Naturally enough, Andrew was puzzled by the business about the blinds. He assumed that the code related to some male threat but agreed to be bound by it. In the course of the conversation she saw two pregnant women passing by, swollen, smocked and smug. She hated them.

Back at work, too late for coffee, sweating and dizzy, she thought of those fat, cruising mothers-to-be and tried to strengthen herself by being the opposite – wiry and working. After all, most women in the world jolly well had to work until the moment baby was born.

It was, however, hard to concentrate on the job. She held out a raincoat for a woman to try.

Do you remember when there was a baby? Do you remember when there was a baby? The image of the dead baby dwelled in her mind.

"I think a size smaller might be better." The woman smiled at her husband. They always wanted smaller sizes, vanity overriding the common sense of leaving room for thick clothes during a stern winter. Throwing the previous one over her arm, she found the equivalent coat in a Size 10 and held it out.

Do you remember when there was a baby? The baby's dead. The link between babies and death was unbroken.

"Thank you, Miss. Yes, I think this one is quite big enough. This trenchcoat, it is the classic Faversham, isn't it?"

"Yes, of course, Madam." *Classic, classic, classic. They are always using that word.* She wanted to say, "We are all classic here, it depends on your point of view." She silently folded the coat and slipped it in the carrier.

Do you remember when there was a baby? Baby, I'm sorry. I don't want to deny you. Question number one. Straight off, they'd ask: Who's the father? I don't want to answer that. Number two: How will I manage? Something like that and I can't even think about it. I have nothing to say. Something might go wrong for us . . . It's better that no one knows. You have no one else to trust but me.

"Here's your coat, Madam. I'll just make out your bill."

By five thirty she felt less tired than she had in the morning. She was tempted by Carol's offer of a drink. A drink would cheer her, but drinking was bad and drinking led to smoking and that was bad. She walked home by a devious route, avoiding Great Marlborough Street, around Soho and then up Charing Cross Road. There was cleaning to do in the flat, weekly beauty treatment: shampoo, shower, shave the legs, creams and nail-cutting. She knew it would make her feel better. She knew she would not do it. She felt unable to do anything, even the things that used to be classed as nothing. She could neither read nor sew, nor even sit. The old dull evenings now seemed like some lost Eden.

It's all relative. It's all relative. Oh, God! Will even this seem good after what's to come? They say the pain of childbirth is terrible. Now I talk to myself. At least I don't talk out loud in the streets like the mad old women – not yet. I think it's coming. She put her head back and looked at the ceiling. "Ha, ha, ha, bloody funny, ha, ha." The tears in her eyes made it necessary to lower her head. "Self-pity, no genuine sadness. It's all relative and on balance this is unwarranted. Pull yourself together, Brown!" And she did. She drank a glass of milk, then washed her hair under the shower. She was sitting, head down, legs apart, brushing all the hair forward in front of the fire when Boswell rang the bell. She pulled her dressing-gown tight across her chest as she showed him up. He was alone.

A glance at the clock showed that it was only eight. She let one blind down.

"I need to take a few things away, nothing of value. I'll give you a receipt."

He took her address book and diary, two pairs of scissors, stationery and other paper and envelopes.

She told him she had been at work all day and asked if the police were any nearer solving the crime.

"We know where to start and we always get there in the end in cases like this. Are you likely to be going out this evening?"

"No. I washed my hair, but not to go out. I'm staying

in." She took two deep breaths. "Do you really think that I had anything to do with it?"

"We follow certain procedures. In the end the whole pattern will emerge. It's not like Sherlock Holmes where I play my violin and meditate. I collect facts and listen and I'll go on doing that until I'm satisfied that I have all the facts and have heard the whole story."

"I see. I can't think of anything else to tell you."

Boswell's face remained impassive. "Have you seen your neighbours today?" She shook her head. "They seem to be out at the moment and they are not giving us much co-operation. We'll be back here later, I expect, but I don't think that we'll have to bother you again tonight. Goodnight, Miss Brown."

The house was silent. Katie sat watching the clock, saw two hours pass, and felt as if she barely existed. 'My reward for being nothing, doing nothing,' she thought bleakly, 'is going to be like this, on and on.' If she were to close her eyes now she knew there were images of rabbits, a baby and death.

Chapter eighteen

His penis was sore, his head was sore. He had had too much to drink when he got in last night. Well, you could hardly blame her, he told himself. He had done the right thing but not expected the violent response. He had expected gentle understanding – it was true she had lost her sense of humour, not surprising, really. He wanted to phone her to resolve the situation, but could not. He must wait. How, then , would it end? He wanted to win, to win her round again. It felt like losing a friend – apart from the sore penis, damn it. He drank his breakfast coffee in one go, went and refilled the cup.

They had caught up with those playmates of Sir Joe of the Home Office, in the child pornography game. It was nearly out in the open, now. The two creatures he was going to see today were certainly part of it. Still, the going could be difficult – impossible, probably – to get to them without dragging the high-and-mighty-recently-departed down as well. There was no go-ahead for that yet. This nasty business, the baby's murder, these things always crop up just before Christmas. He scratched his crotch and yawned.

The BBC news was over, the fast-chatting commentators sounded fatuous, so he retuned to a music programme. 'Mighty Fine' was bopping out. He turned the radio off to go to the bathroom. It would be all right in the end, they would be back to normal once the case was cleared. He reckoned her a reasonable person, more reasonable than most women; only the circumstances were unreasonable.

Yesterday he had gone to an address in Bayswater to interview a man, nasty-looking, a bulbous drinker's nose and large bloodshot eyes. There were 'artistic' studies of boys adorning the walls and lodged in two filing cabinets. Now, looking at his own face in the bathroom mirror, he recalled photographs of himself as a baby and in his childhood. Where was the pleasant fullness, the unblemished skin? He rubbed his chin, recently shaved but still a nodular landscape compared to a child's. His muscles tensed in the endeavour to improve his image. It was difficult to imagine that even the worst of those rogues had once been held by proud, loving mothers – mother's boy, mother's little treasure. Perhaps they had not, and that was the trouble.

Dark-grey suit, white shirt, striped tie, the most routine clothes for a routine day. Routine for bloody routine. He left the flat in a sad temper, wondering whether to take an initiative with a chum of his, a journalist, give him a sniff of scandal relating to no-names-mentioned. It was a worthless gamble if it only left a diffuse feeling of self-righteousness. Pondering on that cheered him somewhat.

Katie was the first to arrive. Faversham's showroom looked like an old stage set for one of those middle-class dramas, a well-lit over-large room, a polished table with its huge floral arrangement, fake eighteenth-century chairs; but the racks of clothes (escaped from the wardrobe department?) ruined the illusion. The flowers never looked quite real, not like a bunch stuck in a pot in an ordinary house. She put her nose to a chrysanthemum, took a deep breath, and felt better all through.

In the changing room she bothered to glance only briefly in the mirror. She combed her hair in a negligent fashion. 'I've changed from a girl who never took a trip without a ton of make-up but forgot the toothbrush to the sort with just toothbrush, soap and woolly vest.' Smiling sadly at the thought, she pulled back the curtain. Marian was standing there, a large comb in her hand. The two women gasped, laughed, then exchanged places.

Katie had reserved her coffee-break to initiate herself into the approved maternal system. She stood in the phone box and received her instructions from the clinic – to bring the doctor's letter and a sample of urine, the first of the morning. It was fixed for nine fifteen next Wednesday morning, which happened to be her day off.

At the lunch-hour the vegetarian restaurant was full of people. She saw one free chair at a table otherwise occupied by two young men.

"Do you mind if I sit here?"

They both rose.

"No, Ma'am, it would be our pleasure," the older one said. He pulled the free chair out as far as he was able in the crowded circumstances.

Settled in and a few mouthfuls eaten, she asked them if they were on holiday.

"Yes, Ma'am. We have been to Rome and to Paris and now we're in England for three days before leaving Europe. This is certainly a very beautiful city."

The two handsome brothers from Texas continued to make polite conversation and utterly entranced Katie. Now she understood what Laurence meant about the charm of the casual acquaintance, uncritical companionship.

Over the years Katie had unconsciously absorbed a part of the Faversham tradition. She had come to terms with the demands, physical and mental, made on a shop assistant in the Ladies' Department. With all the events of recent weeks her attitude to work had changed. She felt she could use her work role as a protection which she would adopt or shed at will. This was a way of managing herself when it seemed impossible to endure all those hours of tiredness, sickness, sadness and having to ask at least seven times a day if she could go up to the lavatory.

Today it was Marian's turn to be upset. Katie saw her coming through the central doors with tears in her eyes. She pulled a small hanky from her sleeve and went into the office. It had happened before: on that occasion, Katie had offered comfort and been rejected. This time she asked Angela what was wrong – a muddle about alteration tickets, not even Marian's fault. It was silly to be so upset. Marian admitted this, but could not help herself – it was for this that she had turned down repeated offers of promotion.

Pam nudged Katie. "Look, he's here!" Fred stood alone, his hands in his raincoat pockets. Katie looked about for Angela, who had gone, no doubt, to talk to Marian.

"Katie, can I see you, please?"

She went up to him. Who cared, she thought, if she was 'Katie' now? Who cared about the whispers behind her?

"I've told Greg Adams that Miss Rufus was picked up this morning. She took forty bikinis from Harrods. Working there under an assumed name. Huh . . . I'm not on the case anymore, anyway. It was you I came to see. To apologise. I'm not saying I was wrong, but I suppose I didn't go about it very well . . . Something like that . . . I suppose you know what I mean."

She shrugged her shoulders and looked straight into his pale-grey eyes. They closed a fraction at the stare, a tiny smile curled his mouth as he leant towards her and whispered in her ear. "My cock's killing me it's so sore."

"I hope it succeeds." The smile left his face. He turned and walked through the doors.

She walked quickly after him. "Come on." Together they slowly descended the stairs, stopping before the bottom landing.

"They think I killed that baby, don't they? In a funny way, I get more and more involved with what went on. The links seem to get stronger."

"As far as I know, they suspect the chauffeur: he has a record. But they have to check even the rank outsiders like yourself. They're in a fix, so they go on and on sifting through what they know."

"Boswell took notepaper and my diary and address book from the flat last night."

"Am I in them?"

"Bloody typical!" She looked away in rage, then glared at him. "I wrote that you are a lousy lover and lots of other very personal details."

He looked shocked, paler than ever, then laughed, less than half-heartedly.

"I'm sorry. It's lousy luck." He put his hands on her shoulders.

"I'm sorry, too." She turned and walked up the stairs. Before turning at the half-landing, she looked back. He was watching her.

Both blinds were up in the front room, the lights were off, the bedroom door was shut, when the bell rang at seven o'clock. Katie peeped out of the corner of the window before going down to open the door for Andrew. She held his hand, hurried him up the stairs, closed and locked the door behind them, led him across the darkened room and into the bedroom, immediately closing and bolting the door.

"What the hell is going on, Katie? Why all the drama?"

She put her arms around his neck, he gave her a long warm kiss, pushed her away and asked, "Come on, tell me. What is this all about?"

"I never told you this before, but I have a husband. He was a wrestler. He's just come out of jail."

Andrew remained silent.

"Darling Andrew. I'm so pleased to see you." She ignored further questions as she undressed him and, with some help, herself.

She felt his penis harden, straddled him, knew the shock of it pushing up inside her. She drove herself decisively up and down until she lost control in a frenzy of vibration. She lifted herself from his sticky body to lie on her back beside him and look straight up to the ceiling.

"They want me for murder," she announced flatly.

"Are you joking?" He rolled on to one side and saw that she was not. "Listen, Katie, if this is serious, you've got to tell me. I could get involved, you know."

He was frightened and looked apprehensive and something in that pleased her. In his own selfish way he was involved. This was a decisive moment, not another wishy-washy compromise.

He was up, sitting on the edge of the bed, pulling on his vest. "Tell me what the hell is going on. Does it have anything to do with those louts who live upstairs?"

"The Italian baby who was kidnapped and murdered in London . . ."

"Yes, I saw it on television last night."

"I didn't listen."

"Why the hell don't you buy a television like everyone else? . . . Sorry." He combed his hair with his fingers. "What has this murder to do with you? Do you really know anything about it?"

"I am involved – that is, I know one member of the family. Well, no. I don't actually know her, we've met, that's all. I thought maybe the people upstairs were connected, it's all coincidences. The police seem to think that I'm involved. Maybe I'm neurotic, imagining things. Maybe they think I'm mad. They keep coming and asking questions and looking around. Oh, God! I'm so fed up with the whole business." She was sobbing and sniffing. "I'm sorry. I just had to see you. I do seem to be going a bit mad. I don't know what to do. Oh, God! What a muddle."

"Come on, Katie. I've never seen you so tense before. You're innocent so you'll be all right. Like you said, it's a muddle. It's just a muddle. But it could be more than a muddle for me, don't you see? You have to see that. I think I'd better go. I shouldn't have come in the first place. For Christ's sake, Katie, the police, the press, everyone could be watching this place by now. I must go." She was not moving, not even crying.

"I hate leaving you like this, honestly."

"You'll be glad to go. You once said that things have to change to remain the same and this affair has gone on and on, one night a week for so long. We can't go to the theatre or the cinema, in case someone sees you. We have to creep into local restaurants, then back here for a quick tumble. It has gone on and on like that for so long. I liked it, really. It couldn't go on being good for you, though. You got bored with it and now you're threatened. I do really need you for once even if we had nowhere to go . . . Go on, go away."

"Katie, listen. You know that I do love seeing you. But it is a big risk for me. I risk my family, my house, my home, most of my income. If my wife finds out, I know she'd divorce me. She would love to have everything we have together without me. She's sick of me."

"Thank you. I know you're trying to make me feel bad, wanting me to blame myself for needing to see you."

"I don't want to live without my children. I know I would end up hating anyone who, however indirectly, took them away from me."

"Thank you, again. I expect I will feel bad about it all tomorrow anyway. Why don't you go? You're dressed for the part."

"Come on, Katie. You have your funny little life." He pulled on the last of his clothes. "Your jolly independent life. I used to annoy you when I criticised your lifestyle, I know. In fact, I suppose if I was free – single again, with a flat in the middle of town – I'd live much as you do."

"You don't know how I live."

"All right. Well, you have nothing to lose . . ." He looked at her impassive face. "By the sound of it, you'd be better off without me."

He bent to kiss her. She turned her head away. Though longing to beg him to come back, she sensed that her instincts were mistaken. The door of the front room was closed quietly, the bedroom door left ajar. There was a long wait before the outside door closed, again very quietly. For an hour she watched the hands of the bedroom clock.

Chapter nineteen

"Pam, you know you said you'd do a late night for me? Could you by any chance stay late tonight? It isn't important if you can't. I just don't feel very well."

"I didn't like to say so, but you are looking pale. Are you losing weight?"

"I always weigh about the same."

"Well, I'll ring my mother. I wasn't doing anything tonight, anyway. I'm trying to stay in a bit before Christmas. They're ever so upset that I'm going away with Bill for the holiday. But I'm twenty-five now – I know my own mind. I know how it is when you feel a bit off-colour. You haven't eaten something have you? You eat a lot of that foreign food, don't you?"

At midday lunch Katie noticed that the owner of the Greasy Spoon was away. She was rather surprised that this minor change should be able to make her feel at all upset. Carol sat opposite, across the narrow table.

"I thought you were slimming, eating at that cranky vegetarian place. I'm glad you didn't try to get me to go there today. I can't stand it, fifty pence for a bowl of uncooked carrots."

They started to fork the chips into their mouths, every two or three chips got dunked into the fried egg yolk before being consumed.

"Forty bikinis! She must be mad. In the middle of winter, as well!" Katie forked in several chips and waited for a reply.

"I don't know how shops take people on without checking references and tax forms and all that."

"An Italian friend of mine got a job at Claridges: interview one day, cleaning Kissinger's bedroom the next – that was when he was American Secretary of State."

"I may be thick, but I do know who Kissinger is."

"Sure. But what you don't know and Claridges didn't either is that my friend was connected with an extreme leftist group and started planning an assassination immediately."

"Well, what happened?"

"Nothing. She started planning too late."

"That reminds me," said Carol. "Diane, she's in Holloway now, you know, awaiting trial."

"I wonder what you get for your lunch there?"

"I bet the chips are better. Let's face it, they couldn't be much worse."

About half Katie's helping lay rejected on the plate. She had put aside those burnt-hard and brown or blemished ones. The tea ordered to wash away the worst effects of the food had developed a film of marbled cream on its surface; nevertheless, she drank it down easily – it was nearly cold.

"It's sad to think of her locked in a cell. I wonder what she's thinking about now? Do you imagine she's full of regrets?"

"Only for being caught," Carol snorted. "She did have her chances, let's face it. The rest of us have to scrape along on miserable wages. She took the risk and she lost."

"I suppose you're right. Let's get out of here – it's so hot I'm burning up. I feel sick."

Every detail of those chips haunted Katie during that afternoon. She chided herself, tried to divert herself, but no action or thought took the nauseating memory away. Tea at half past three, she told herself, knowing that the tea would taste of potatoes, grease and tomato. It was no good. It must have been at the back of her mind all the time, that today she would leave early. She told Angela that she felt ill, that she was going to be sick. She left.

Only yards from the shop she suddenly realised that she felt fine; considered stopping off for a tea on the way home, but decided that it was not a time for treats and hurried on. As soon as she opened the front door she heard footsteps on the stairs. With the door open as wide as possible and two bags of rubbish and a pram in the entrance hall, Katie stood just inside as the girl walked slowly down towards her.

Black shiny shoes, grey stockings, a grey flannel skirt and above the simple shirt was the same maroon cravat. The longish hair was held back at one side with a slide, her cheeks just a little pink. Katie was in the way.

"Are you just coming in? I'm sorry . . ."

Katie moved to allow them to pass. As soon as the girl reached the pavement she turned to see if her escort was still there. He, too, apologised to Katie in a polite, public-school voice. They briskly walked off, side by side.

It had to be the same girl. It was Andrew's girlfriend. I would swear it in court. I should ring Boswell. Is this case intimately linked with everyone in my life? But Andrew certainly does not want to have anything to do with it. (Who would volunteer an interest in a murder case?) Those two are not the sort to be the Remers' friends. They're not the sort of people who sell insurance or hire out televisions, nor are they social workers. Boswell will think I have a persecution complex. Why persecute me? I'm just too unimportant and boring and yet there is persecution – by the Remers, by the police and now by Andrew? The girl? Myself?

She made a pot of tea and put four digestive biscuits on the tray. She huddled next to the fire. *So many coincidences, there can't be many more to come. Yet only more will let me understand what's going on. They have to be only coincidences: the lavatory in Great Marlborough Street, a sudden whim. Seeing Andrew and the girl in Sandra's when I had changed my lunch-time with Lotte. Coming home early today. No one could predict any of them. It can't be possible that I'll ever know what's going on. It can't be possible that I'll ever understand what's happening. Soon, I'll be totally on my own. Is that what the police, the courts, the asylums do? They explain it for you, they make it into a pattern, a design for the mad.* She wished she had a better brain, could see it from another angle – laterally, perhaps. Then she coughed on a biscuit crumb. From then on every time she ate, even a speck, she coughed out a spray of crumbs. It could be funny, she told herself. Cough, cough. Now her eyes were wet with tears and she a tiny mind hardly part of the great syncopating mass of her body as it sobbed, chuckled, coughed and cursed in repeated sequence.

The cider worked well as a medicine. She drank several glasses and felt not quite fine, but strangely better. No one called. There was nothing possible to do, so she drank and smoked on. As the drink started to make her feel queasy, remorse took over. She walked up and down talking to herself, or rather to her baby-self:

I'm not mad, but what's going on is mad – so it's close. They can say that I'm mad and if I tell it all in some ways, yes, I am mad. They'll take you away from me – your mad mother. I have no money, anyway. You have no father, nothing. When I think of you like that, I seem able to love you more: the more you lack, the more real you seem. Perhaps the seeds of madness have always been present. Forgive me – right now I love you.

It seemed as pointless as anything else, but at least going to bed would put an end to the smoking and drinking. It was midnight, anyway. She would keep to the outward conventions, cling to her mundane image. They would not beat her. She knew that the glory of insanity was a myth. Teeth cleaned, face washed, she straightened a clean sheet over the bed, tucked it in, curled up under the duvet and waited for the warmth of the body to do its work.

A continuous ringing of a bell was the thread that led her back to consciousness. Hammering on the front door confirmed the reality of the present. Crash, another crash and bang. The door broke open in the hall below. Feet pounded the stairs and along the corridor outside her bedroom, up the next flight to the corridor above. More hammering above, another crash, shouts and a scuffle. Thuds on the downward journey, but a slower descent with something heavy being dragged. There were voices – loud but indistinct, muffled.

"Wrongful arrest . . . nothing to do with us . . . It's the fault of the bitch who lives here . . . Leave my wife and the kid out of this . . ." A baby whimpering, a woman's voice sobbing, "Oh, no. Please, no."

Silence.

She got up, put on her dressing-gown and went to look over the banister: the front door was open, shattered around the lock, jagged pale splinters of wood fringing a strip of black paint. The light in the front room seemed too bright, surreal. The littered ashtray and glass still sat on the table. She poured herself some cider and lit a cigarette . . . The entire haunted house was quiet and seedy, but all hers.

There were footsteps on the stairs and a knock on the door. Glass in hand, she opened the door and, with a surge of relief she had not been aware of needing, found a breathless Fred Anchor standing quite straight and pale. She stood back to allow him in.

"I was just about to go to bed when I heard the news. I had asked them to keep me informed – because they knew that I know you." He pushed his glasses up his nose like a punctuation mark – all was explained.

"No one has told me the news," she said drily. "Would you like some cider? I've had a bit too much already."

"That's too bad, I'm sorry. I expect they'll be along soon. I guess they're tied up at the moment. Anyway, it can't do any harm to tell you now. I could do with a drink, thanks." He drank thirstily. "There was some sort of tip-off from the outside, then the chauffeur blew the story and they came and picked up our chums from upstairs."

"I've heard that before."

"So you do know what happened?"

"No. 'A tip-off from outside' – that's what Greg Adams said about the robbery in the shop." She shook her head. "Sorry. Tell me again. I don't understand."

He looked concerned, but drew breath and resumed the tale. "Well, it seems that the chauffeur and the bloke from upstairs here were pals from way back – only we didn't know that until today. That was the tip-off. They planned it all together. The fact that you lived in the same house and knew the family was purely coincidental: it led to a reunion of villains, that's all."

"What about the public lavatory? Was that coincidental as well?"

"What do you mean?"

"I went to that same loo on the day the baby was found there."

"Did you tell anyone that?"

"No, but I'm telling you now." She shrugged her shoulders and poured more cider into the shared glass.

135

They sipped it in turns. 'What about Andrew's girl-friend's visit?' she puzzled silently.

"I suppose it's just possible Remer was following you, or saw you. If he's none too bright he might have hoped to incriminate you. Boswell will get the truth out of our chums."

"Are we all 'your chums', once we're criminals?"

He sighed and shook his head. "It's only a manner of speaking."

She closed her eyes and rubbed her forehead upwards with the fingers of one hand.

Fred answered a knock at the door and went out on to the landing. Katie heard lowered voices and resented the fact that he was dealing with her business. She felt that she had to remain completely in control if she was ever to understand what had happened. She wondered if her life could ever return to what it had been. Maybe that was impossible – indeed, undesirable. For an objective view she could consult Laurence: a glance from the window showed that he was either in bed or out. Her energy had no outlet. She rubbed her hands together and lit another cigarette. Maybe it was all over, maybe not. She was still agitated – the story might have yet another twist. So it was, whichever way she looked at it.

"That was the police again," announced Fred, returning. "They are mending the door now. The couple upstairs have been charged. He's on three charges: unlawful imprisonment, murder – that may have to be reduced to manslaughter – and demanding money with menace. She's an accomplice on all counts, as well as the chauffeur, Brian Carstairs."

"What will happen to the baby? To their baby, Brendan?"

"Well, he'll stay with her for the time being at least, certainly. He'll be looked after. It may be better for him in the long run."

"I doubt it." There were tears in her eyes.

He came around the table and put an arm over her shoulder.

"You've been magnificent." He lifted her gently and she rose reluctantly to allow him to kiss her. Downstairs there was hammering. Their bodies pressed together, he brushed away her tears.

When the policemen came upstairs she pulled her dressing-gown around herself. She opened the door a crack.

"The door's fixed now, Miss. You'll be all right for the time being, but it will need mending properly. If you ring the station, they'll tell you about compensation, but it's quite safe for the present."

"Thank you very much."

Turning, she saw that Fred had taken his jacket off. He looked like a stranger. It might as well have been the other policeman standing there. She needed comfort. She returned to Fred's embrace.

As they lay in each other's arms she listened, saying nothing.

"Katie, I missed you so much. I thought about you all the time. I couldn't get you out of my mind. I dreamt about this moment, when we'd be together again. I don't think I've ever missed anyone so much in my whole life. Don't let what has happened spoil it." He drew back and looked at her. There was no reply. "Tell me what you're thinking, whatever it is, please."

She was thinking that his thoughts were exactly those she had about Andrew. It was nice to hear them, even from someone else.

"I don't know what to think, really," she replied, softly.

He looked sad, then went back to caressing her. They made love deliberately and gently. She felt the blood move around her body again. It seemed to ease and then excite all of her, even her mind. When it was over, they stayed together side by side. She felt her face pink and glowing. It was a funny little miracle that she had not expected to work.

"I can't bear it, you not saying anything like this. Are you still annoyed with me? I don't blame you. It will be all right. Oh, my darling, thank you." He kissed her again.

She smiled at him. "I can't just slip back into the old ways. I suppose it will come all right in the end." She knew that was a lie. Now she wanted to tell him about being pregnant. She did not. Did she want to punish him? Not really. She wanted more drama, she had become accustomed to it, but was clinging to the old habit of being secretive. Anyway, soon enough he would know. *Soon, no more Andrew, no more Fred?* The thought had a gentle charm.

Chapter twenty

At seven in the morning rain was falling steadily. Could Katherine in her prison cell hear it? Katie hoped Brendan was warm and comforted. Fred stirred, turned and put out his arm. She snuggled alongside. They were perfectly suited by size, her toes next to his, her body against his and their mouths meeting. The bed retained the shared tastes and warm smells of the night.

"What's the time?"

"It's only seven."

"Great, I don't suppose you've got a razor here, have you?"

"I don't shave every day, but I do own a razor. You can use it if you promise not to be rude about it."

She went to the kitchen, washed the glass and ashtray and cleaned the sink so that he could shave. She boiled water and made a large pot of coffee. Her shower only took five minutes, then she took a tray back to bed. Fred was sleeping again.

At eight he was up, wearing her dressing-gown. The doorbell rang. It took her a minute or so to put on clothes and go downstairs to the door. It was Andrew. He immediately wanted to step inside out of the pouring rain. She stood in his way, saying, "I'm just going to work. I've hardly slept." He knew – she felt sure he knew – that someone else was up there. *Just my luck. The only time for months there has been someone here and the only time for years that he has called in the morning. Damn it!* She wanted him to come up, for them to be friends, open with each other again. If Fred were already dressed she could have contemplated asking Andrew in, to introduce them to each other. However, a sordid row or sticky silence were not needed so early in the day. The polite, final drama should be postponed.

"I came to see if you are all right. Can I come up for a minute?" He studied the crudely repaired door.

"No." She replied.

"Well, that's gratitude for you . . . I'll be seeing you."

"Listen, please ring me at work. Please! Or I could ring you."

"Suit yourself."

She walked slowly up the stairs and back into the room. Fred turned nervously. He was fully dressed, in the centre of the room. They stared at each other.

"A friend of mine. People are worried for me." She attempted a smile, went through to the bedroom and sat before the mirror, the warmth of the morning lost.

Fred took her in his car to the shop, the rain streaming down the windscreen, inside steamy. Alongside the shop he put a hand on her knee.

"Can I take you out for dinner tonight, young woman?"

"No, I have to see a friend."

"Are you booked up for the weekend as well?"

"I'm working on Saturday, otherwise I don't have any plans."

"OK. I'll pick you up at seven on Saturday."

They kissed briefly and she left to rush through the rain to the staff door. Pam stood inside, folding an umbrella.

"You are lucky having a lift on a morning like this. Are you feeling better? Did you find out what was wrong?"

"I think I must have eaten something. Maybe it was the chips at lunch-time."

'Brighten up!' Katie was to tell herself several times that day, as routine prolonged routine. The brightness she felt was surface gleam, like ice on a murky puddle. The elation of waking early was soon negated by the lack of sleep underlain by the continual nausea. In the old days if she missed a period she offered a desperate trade-off: If only I'm not pregnant, I'll be good, careful, sensible, grateful for ever and ever. Today's bargain: Please let it be a healthy child. I will give up smoking and drinking, I will be good, only let it be all right.

In the course of the morning she told the others the rough outline of the baby murder and her involvement in the case.

"No wonder you've been looking a bit peaky. I don't know how you coped. Was that detective involved? Professionally, I mean. Fancy knowing people who could do a thing like that!"

"Well, they weren't exactly Katie's friends, Pam," put in Marian, adding a plea for the restoration of the death penalty.

Katie felt different. *No more hanging. Thank God.*

"Listen, I'm sorry, but I really don't want to talk about it anymore."

They all understood, they said. The first coffee-breaks of the day had started.

"I would say that such people should be beaten."

"Lotte, she doesn't want to hear any more about it now. Can you see to this customer?" Angela sat down as Lotte rose. "If you need any time off, for the police or anything like that, it will be quite all right, I'm sure. I'll mention it to Mr Gain." Katie thanked her. She wondered if her image had been soiled even further by this latest episode. Nevertheless she smiled: it was a tidy excuse to take time off for the hospital or whatever. *What an awful thought. A little murder provides a tidy excuse.*

She wanted to ring Laurence. Her request was granted without a flicker of a frown.

"Katie, don't tell me you've got a job at the National Theatre? No. With the police then? OK, I give up. Why the phone call? . . . An invitation to dinner . . . I'm free . . . It's not going to be your moussaka again, is it? . . . Who else is invited? . . . Only the pleasure of my own company? . . . All right, I won't wear that jacket . . . Have you come into some money then? . . . I'll wait and see . . . See you tonight."

She did not have the time to be tired. By seven she was dressed and ready when Laurence appeared bathed and smart for his treat. They entered the restaurant in the quiet of the early evening. The maître d'hôtel showed them to a table upstairs by the window. The window was kept closed but the scene outside was familiar to them both: the restaurant was only just around the corner.

"A drink before your meal?" The waiter asked.

Laurence ordered an Irish whiskey with water. Katie asked for the wine list. She would stick to wine.

"Are you sure you can afford this, Katie?"

"No. But what the hell."

"Oh, well, it's your funeral – if you'll excuse the expression."

"I've asked you here tonight to thank you for the other day. Now I can explain what was going on – at least, most of what was going on."

With an interruption or two for ordering the food

and wine, she told him all there was to tell.

A stray tear fell absurdly into her lobster bisque.

"Oh, God, I was such a fool. I never made the connection. I only remembered afterwards that I had seen Alan Remer with the chauffeur. It was nothing, just asking him for a light or some such thing. When I noticed the baby swap, that was different: I was drunk, we'd just come from The Weymouth. I did tell Boswell, but it was too late by then. I could have saved the baby if I hadn't been so slow, so stupid."

"But how does Andrew's girlfriend fit into it? And the public lavatory? That's creepy. You'd better ask your Inspector. The mistakes you made, if they were mistakes, were perfectly natural mishaps. If it hadn't been for you, the Remers would still be at large. Think of that."

"Think of what? Being the cause of the whole bloody business? Remer only met the chauffeur when Tamara called at my flat . . . Mishaps, coincidences and murder. What a way to run a life!"

She told the waiter to take the soup away. He needed assurance that there was nothing wrong with it. They each had a Dover sole placed in front of them. Katie's was covered in creamy sauce and peeled grapes. Laurence's was singed brown, shiny with butter and speckled with parsley.

"Did you know that Sole Meunière was the only food poor old Proust could keep down during the last months of his life? He worked through the nights, resting during daylight, confined to a cork-lined room by an asthmatic allergy to pollen."

"Couldn't he eat madeleines?"

"Gosh, it's good. With Dover soles, who needs madeleines?"

Laurence scoffed his food. Katie picked at hers, dutifully trying to feed the baby although not wanting the stuff herself. The wine, a 1975 Meursault, went down all too easily. Half-way, she ordered another bottle.

"Do you know the only true universal language?"

"I'm sure you'll tell me. I don't think I know anything."

"You just lack intellectual curiosity at present. Go on, try . . ." He waited. "Anyway, it's infants' babble. They all use the same words, Chinese, Eskimos, New Yorkers, the lot of them. Don't you think that's fascinating?"

"I don't really want to hear anything about babies right now."

"Also," Laurence continued undeterred, "I think there are other universal languages – body movements, emotional responses, and so on."

"They're not languages. Are you saying that we're all babies in some way, underneath it all?"

"Only, I suppose, that there must be some basic sympathy between humans." Katie gave a disparaging sniff, but Laurence was not going to stop. "Words are misunderstood, even in a shared culture. I doubt that history will prove the wisdom of babies. They're totally selfish, of course. Trouble in any language . . . All right, what about the next election?"

"Oh, shut up, you babbling tot! Call the waiter and ask for some cigarettes for me."

He signalled to the waiter and gave the order.

"Oral fixation, cigarettes. Unfinished infant business, don't you know? All right, here you are." He took the box off the offered tray. The waiter waited for the money to replace the pack and Laurence supplied it. Katie leant across the table and pushed a crumpled pound note into his top pocket.

"Rich today, gone tomorrow!"

"What do you want for Christmas this year, Katie,

dear. Get your order in now, you've weakened me with wine."

A big bloody period, blood stains, lots of blood clots, piles of towels and tampons. Satisfaction for my blood lust. I want to run down the street, my hands covered and dripping in scarlet, like Lady Macbeth: but I'd never wash it off. Suddenly she remembered where she was; she was so drunk by now she thought for a moment that she had said the words out loud. Now should she tell him, share the joyless news with her friend? Again she decided no.

"Well? This is your last chance. What's it to be?"

"A bottle of wine."

"Done. As long as you don't share it with that awful Scot."

"Mind your own business. Please ask for the bill. I don't think I can stand up."

Chapter twenty-one

"After thirty times you have to dry the sheets out."

"And you believed them? Who was she again?"

"An old college chum. They were counting, so I had to believe them."

"Well, I'm knackered after . . . how many times did you say it was? . . . I reckon half a dozen is enough. My personal best! Don't tell me you want more. There must be something wrong with you."

"Oh, I just lie there thinking of England and the CID. It just keeps building up and it's always different. But if you're not up to it . . ."

"Sometimes you might just try lying there. Come here, Katie." Fred pulled her on to his lap and put his arms around her.

Outside it was dark. She had glided through Sunday without the auto-pilot of habit: no time, no clothes, no familiar surroundings, repeated love-makings, feelings surging on and off – freedom, but finally, now, a sense of nothingness and a slow desire to return to the normal world. She sipped hot tea, there was a baby inside hurting her with hunger. She ached to be alone, her own private person with her own private familiar. If only she could find a balance between love and friendship, the ordinary pottering-about surface of life as well as the deeper strange things where you lose your separate state.

Then it occurred to her that it kept coming and

going, like the desire today: love was like that, her love for Andrew – it came and went a hundred times a day. Why had she not realised that before now? She felt as if she had solved one of life's great mysteries. The certainty led to doubt and she concluded by thinking that someone like Pam, who at twenty-five knew her own mind, had probably known this for years already. She would say, of course, "Well, this is it."

"You don't really want to go back to your flat, do you?"

From his tone, it might have been 'your place' or even 'your dump' instead of 'flat'.

"Let's go and have a meal first, anyway. We've hardly eaten at all today, I'm starving."

They ate Dim Sum snacks with tea at a Chinese restaurant on his patch. By the time they had finished, the pubs were open and they drank beer before he left her safely installed at home.

It was cold in the flat and she wondered quite why she had chosen to come back. She still felt sensual. Sensuality breeds sensuality. Again, she could not settle to sew or to read. Instead, she listened to the radio, fell asleep on the sofa and eventually summoned up enough energy to go to bed, alone and nearly herself again.

Fred considered more beer but drove instead, without really thinking, to his flat. The place retained some feeling of the day's events. A sense of them. It was warm, of course, with voices and the buzz of movement only just absent. He poured himself a whisky and sat down. Remembering the love-making made him smile. Funny woman, she seemed to have known in some ways the sordid part of life but to have remained unsullied by any of it. She did not seem to be making a great effort to please him. It all seemed honest and straightforward, it all fitted for him. He doubted that it seemed so right for her. She could just move in here with him, that's the way these things happen nowadays, between two adults. He had always assumed it would be like the old days for him with parents and engagements and the like. In a way, that had been easier. It was dictated and had a settled pattern. What was he to do now? It could only happen naturally, if it was going to. He felt frustrated, he wanted to be able to act – to make something happen. He smiled again at the thought of women's liberation, but now it was upon him. She was independent, she was not going to need him in the old sense. He felt a certain satisfaction in the knowledge that this was like the media. He was creating a myth to match another myth and also being pleasingly different from his colleagues. It had to be a better way, it was evolution. He still felt uncomfortable. He had to be careful, but not look too deliberately casual nor too set on achieving some goal. It was all natural and unself-conscious – it was evolution.

Tomorrow he would finish the final report on the Laskey case. He turned on the television and watched a nature programme. Marvellous, he thought, a colour television better than a university. It was exciting, so much to see and to learn in the world . . .

Chapter twenty-two

"Mrs Brown, please!"

She rose from the long line of seated swollen women to enter a curtained cubicle.

"*Miss* Brown," she told the nurse.

"Yes. Well, go on through and take your clothes off; you'll find a gown in there. Give me your sample. The doctor's letter? Thank you. Off you go."

The white coat accentuated the velvet dusky skin. Tall and thin, his head bent over the open file, he looked like a heron bird. As he turned, smiling to meet her gaze, his gold-rimmed spectacles glinted.

"I'm Doctor Rushdie, Mr Irons's registrar. He will come and see you in a few minutes." He swung around the curtain, his white coat flapping behind him.

The edge of the barely padded table was cold against her nakedness. She slid off and stood to inspect the instruments set out on the glass-topped trolley.

"Good morning, Mrs Brown." There was disapproval in the voice. She perched herself on the padded table again. Mr Irons, suitably grey-suited, with grey hair and grey eyes behind black-framed spectacles, stood gazing down at her. She thought it unlikely that he remembered their previous meeting when she had been desperate to rid herself of a foetus.

"Let's have a look at you, shall we?" He was pulling on a pair of thin plastic gloves. The sister standing at the end of the table told Katie to undo her gown, lie on

149

her side and bend her knees. She edged away from the probing hand. He was looking down at the floor, nodding and murmuring to himself as his cold hard fingers worked away inside her.

"Would you mind if another doctor examines you as well?"

She said no. He called for Doctor Rushdie to come back. The registrar took his turn at probing. "Well, what do you think?" The consultant asked Rushdie.

"About four months." He turned Katie over and pushed down in a few places on her tummy. "Very little swelling. It's difficult to be sure . . ."

"Yes." Irons looked down at Katie. "When was your last period?" He turned and looked at the form and then back to her. "June . . . You've been a bit silly, you know. At your age – what are you now? Thirty-five and with your history, you should have come here much earlier. I'm going to send you for a scan and a blood test. This is all routine, but you should really have had an amniocentesis. I suppose you know there's a greater statistical likelihood of your having a Downs Syndrome baby at your age. Are you still working? What's your usual weight? I see. Well, I'm going to ask you to come back next week. The nurse will tell you about the tests. Good morning." Irons left briskly. The young doctor managed a quick farewell grin in pursuit of his superior. Katie laughed off the effect of the grin: this was surely both the time and place to quit those jolly games.

Dabbing a wisp of cotton-wool against the vein in her arm, Katie found her way to the Ultra Sound Section. The scanners were merry folk and might have been making chocolate commercials, they giggled so much. Gowned anew and with a large glassful of water to swell her up, Katie was stretched under the substantial apparatus, her tummy generously smeared with grease. A pointed arm, which acted as the eye of the device, tentatively criss-crossed her belly. An image appeared on a small screen next to the bed. Katie twisted her neck to see. There was a resemblance to the satellite weather pictures she had seen on television. The woman operator pointed out what she said was an abdomen which was followed by a curious moment, when she saw her insides as a bloated slug doing a somersault. Like a quick-sketch artist, the operator made scribbling movements up, down and across Katie's tummy. "There he is. Come on, young Fred, stop moving about. He's a lively one, this one. I don't think I've seen quite such an active chap before." Katie felt a surge of pride. She could see the little Mickey Mouse figurine flailing around. A doubt crept in: Was it signalling for help?

Despite the high technology the next vital tool was a short length of wire. They pressed a button which held a picture, then measured the head and the abdomen with the wire. Notes were made.

"Is it all right? Can you tell if it's a boy or a girl?"

"We call them all Fred up here. Do you really want to know the sex? It's only really certain if you have an amnio. You've not had one, have you?" The operator looked down at the notes. "Most mums don't want to know. Wouldn't you like a surprise? Are you sure you want to know? Anyway, which is it you want, M or F?"

"I don't care, and it's too late to care, anyway. I don't see why you shouldn't tell me if you can – after all, it's more important to me than to anyone else, isn't it?" Her evident lack of humour puzzled the operator.

"Well, don't quote me on this, but I think it's a boy. See here . . ." She pointed to a blur on the screen. "It's a scrotum . . . wouldn't you say?" She looked to her assistant, who nodded confirmation. "Otherwise, he looks just fine. How far gone are you?" Katie told her.

"Yes, well, he's a lively little mite. Can you feel him moving yet?" Katie said not. The operator closed the folder and turned the machine off.

Chapter twenty-three

He does exist. Katie cooked spaghetti and broccoli for lunch. *He does exist.* She tried to recall those misty outlines. She remembered the activity. She would need to keep it in mind and try never to poison him. Him. Well, it had never occurred to her it would be a boy. As far as she was able, she had imagined it as another one like her. Now she was glad he was him, different from her, from her mother, her sister: they had always been a family of females. He stood a better chance now he was different. There would be fewer preconceptions.

Baby, your father's all right, he's fine in his own way. Maybe you'll know him one day. He does love children, but he can't love you like he does the others. You're better than those others; it's just your bad luck having me for a mother. We'll sort it out, I promise.

Katie focused her attention on the telephone. Andrew, after all, was her habit. A habit, by definition, is difficult to break. She, perhaps, could hope to ease out, away from it. She picked up the receiver and dialled Andrew's office number, not sure whether it should be for the last time, or nearly. After an unusually brief pause, Andrew's voice replied. Yes, he said, he would pop by for a quick drink. When she had replaced the receiver, Katie needed to remind herself that there was nothing to be too pleased about. She curled up on the sofa for the delicious luxury of an afternoon sleep. She was woken by the front-door bell.

Believing, in a dazed fashion, that Andrew had taken to drinking at tea-time, she padded downstairs in her slippers to open the door. Boswell, the Detective Chief Superintendent, had turned away from her door, apparently believing that she was not at home.

"I'm sorry that we haven't been along earlier to see you, Miss Brown. We did call, in fact, last week – but you must have been at work."

"Oh, I see. Do you want to come in?"

Without saying anything, he made it plain that he expected to enter and followed her up the stairs.

"You may, I expect, have realised that we will need you in court. I would like you to jot down a few notes for yourself, dates and so forth."

"Certainly. If you think it will help."

"Don't learn any speeches or anything like that. It's just that we can all forget, and that doesn't help anyone."

"I suppose you have enough evidence against the Remers?"

"My guess is that they'll plead guilty and save us all a lot of trouble. It goes without saying that we owe a lot to you and, of course, we're all extremely grateful for your assistance."

"About the Remers, what made you arrest them in the end?"

"We found the connection between Brian Carstairs, who, as you remember, was the chauffeur, and your neighbour Alan Remer. Once we let Carstairs know that – plus, I must admit, a tiny fiction – we told him that Remer had said more than he had. Then Carstairs broke down and told us all. It was in the bag."

"Did they kill the baby?"

"We don't deal in morals. That's a question for the court to decide. As the press reported, the Anselmo baby died of pneumonia."

"I know. I heard."

"We don't, thank goodness, often have to deal with babies. If the victim had been older, it would have been a different story."

"A happier ending."

"Yes. Like your stories here." He looked to the shelves. "Now you can get back to reading."

"I suppose so," she said doubtfully, shrugging her shoulders. More questions remained unanswered than answered. Unable to think how to begin to find out, the uncertainty left her without anything to say.

After Boswell had left, she mentally framed a number of innocent questions. She really had not understood too much.

"So, you're allowing me past this time," commented Andrew, with a smile. Despite everything, looking at his face she wanted to kiss him. They only kissed once or twice on the way up the stairs, not on every stair. Once inside her room, he held her firmly at arm's length.

"You do know that I can't stay. I'm only here for a few minutes."

"Yes." She kissed him again.

"Well, young Katie, you're more cheerful today."

"And how's your girlfriend?"

For an instant his face fell and the colour changed a shade. "You are my girlfriend. What are you on about? You can't go on living in a world of conspiracies, you know."

He took his raincoat off and turned to put it on the sofa.

"The young one with long straight hair. Looks a bit county for you, I thought."

"How the hell do you know about her? Clare . . .

She's a research assistant. We work together."

"Research work, eh?"

"Come here, Katie." He took her arm again and sat her down next to him on the sofa. "If you must know – I did have an affair with her." Katie smiled and waited. "It was a mistake. Now it's over. She was much too young for me, or rather," he gave a resigned smile, "I was too old for her. She's a fine girl. We went out for a couple of weeks, that's all. I was flattered. She saw me as a big important father figure, I suppose. It's over, like I said." His head hung a little.

Katie kissed him gently on the cheek. "Poor Andrew."

"Have you got a drink?"

"I've got some whisky here, for you."

Without turning to look at him, she went to the table to pour him a drink. "Why did she come here?"

"You know about that!"

She handed him the glass. He took a large gulp.

"I knew, that is, I thought that those bastards upstairs were up to no good. You were in a terrible state. Can I have another dram?"

She rose, refilled the glass and brought it back to him.

"It was worth a try. I sent Clare along with another researcher. She wasn't to be alone with them. It's well known that people tell television interviewers more than they tell their own mothers . . . or the police, for that matter. It's obscene, they'd tell us anything for a chance to get on the box . . . You're not drinking?"

"I don't feel like it. Go on, what did Clare ask them?"

"She gave them some cock and bull story. Poor Clare, she didn't know it was a sham – poverty in modern Britain. She was briefed: questions about childhood, any criminal record. You know the sort of stuff, it's on every week – for those of us who have a television, of course."

"So?" She clasped his hand eagerly.

"So . . . reams of self-pity and the fact that he once spent six months in Borstal. I rang the police and told them that he had a record. That's about all I have to report, Ma'am."

"You didn't say who you were?"

"Certainly not! I was sweating in a call box. You have stood up to it well, considering the pressure you must have been under."

"They told me it was a tip-off from outside."

Andrew was looking at his watch. "Christ, I must go." He stood up. "Admit it, you didn't believe that I was going to help you?"

"Perhaps I should thank Clare as well!"

He stared at her seriously. "I begin to feel as if I have two wives . . . I've got trouble at home . . . I'm getting myself into a real state."

"Have another drink."

"I'm late already. I really do have to rush now. Listen, we must talk. I'll call you to arrange to have lunch some time next week. All right?" Already he had his coat on.

She stood up and hugged him. "Thank you."

A final kiss. The door closed. She watched from the window; he did not look up. The car started and sped off.

The doorbell rang again. Katie rushed down the stairs, opened the door, expecting to see Andrew. Instead, like driving into a brick wall, she was confronted by a rigid Fred Anchor.

"Yes. I waited till your friend left. I just thought it might interest you to know that another of your friends, Greg Adams, has been picked up. My chaps found his flat full of, shall we say, unpaid-for

Faversham clothes. But I expect you know that already."

"What on earth do you mean?"

"He seems to have known you rather well by his account."

"And you believed *him*?" Fred was glaring at her. "Don't stand in the street. Come upstairs and let's talk it over."

"I'm not sure you don't have enough company already." Nevertheless, he entered and followed her up the stairs.

"Why don't you sit down?" she asked, pulling a chair out from the table. "Surely you must realise Adams was trying to get back at you?"

He picked up the glass Andrew had used, sniffed, then replaced it. "I think I'd better sit down. I'm trying to stop myself wanting to hit you."

'If only you knew,' she thought. 'Don't tell him now . . . not for the moment.' But she felt in a weird state, as though anything might happen. 'Finalities are false,' she concluded to herself.

Fred took off his spectacles and wiped his eyes with the backs of his hands.

Katie was too frightened to comfort him.

Finally, he spoke quite gently. "Come here." She came to stand in front of his chair. He put his arms round her waist, resting his head on her hard belly. "I'm sorry."

"I'm sorry, too." She knelt down and kissed his damp hands.

"Of course I don't believe that shit, Adams. I believe in you," he murmured.

Calm and sure, her head resting on his thigh, she sensed warmth and that the warmth was separate from her. It no longer seemed to matter to Katie what he thought of her. A calm, blank divide.

Katie stood up, moved across the room, and sat on the sofa. From now on she belonged to herself and the nothingness was over. A gentle energy invigorated her thoughts. Calmly, yet rapidly, she reviewed what confronted her. The easy lies, the convenient pity for Andrew, and now for Fred. There was no purpose in any more of this. To extinguish the pain it had to be lived through, felt and real.

She lit a cigarette, then stubbed it out. A pattern of life had shifted and she was being driven onwards. By some instinct, she was able to relax – and anyway reason dictated that the moment for choice was past. Katie and the Mickey Mouse figurine, a whirling micro-Fred, were going to be all right. Of that she was absolutely certain.